Gears

of

Golgotha

By

Rebekah McAuliffe

Printed in the United States of America

ISBN: 1942212119
ISBN-13: 978-1-942212-11-9

Hydra Publications
1310 Meadowridge Trail
Goshen, KY 40026

www.hydrapublications.com

Dedication

For Amy.

CHAPTER ONE

"Happy birthday to you." Mother and Father turned out the lights. Their off-key song echoed throughout the small house. "Happy birthday to you. Happy birthday, dear Erin." Father carried a small birthday cake, adorned with butter cream icing and red frosting roses. On top was a lone candle, its flame illuminating the dark room.

"Happy birthday to you." The tongue of fire licked my face as Father set down the cake. My small, thin lips opened into a wide smile, showing off my dimples.

"Blow out the candle, dear," Mother said. I leaned over the cake and closed my eyes. *I wish...*

"Erin, dear," Mother interjected. "Don't you think that making a wish over a candle is illogical?"

"One does not place faith in silly superstitions," Father added.

I sighed. "I guess you're right." I blew out the candle, slightly disappointed. My parents applauded then turned on the lights, revealing the rest of the house.

The room my parents had gathered in was a small dining room and kitchenette. A compact microwave hung above a gas stove. A bulky refrigerator was set up at the corner of the room, leaving just enough space for one person to cook at the stove. My father had found a yellowed lace cover, which he laid across our plain, metal table in an attempt to make our house feel more like a home. The ugly, piss-colored yellow of the appliances blended well with the dilapidated walls of the kitchen.

"The Chemists at The Lab said happy birthday," Father said as he cut himself a piece of the yellow cake. He probably didn't need it, judging from the size of his stomach.

"Now, now, Tom," Mother chastised. Despite the gentleness in her voice, her green eyes threw daggers at Father. "We promised we wouldn't talk about work. Tonight, we are celebrating our little girl growing up to be a beautiful woman."

Father sighed, his already silver hair seeming to gray even more at the news. "You're right." He took a bite of the cake. "This is Erin's night," he said with his mouth full of dessert. "There's no harm in telling her that people are wishing her a happy birthday though. Besides, she's twenty-one now. Like you said, she is growing up. Soon, she'll begin working with us at The Lab. We won't have to deal with those—"

"Tom!" Mother scolded. "Just eat your cake and be quiet." She turned to me, her gnarled hand gently stroking my hair. "Do not worry, dear. Work this week has been hard on your father."

"You're damn right it's been hard," Father said as he stuffed another bite of cake into his mouth. His face was almost as white as his laboratory jacket. "Those damned Mages have done nothing but protest outside the construction sites all week. We Chemists are only trying to make New Pangaea a cleaner, better place. And what do they do all day? Smoke the very thing they're trying to protect."

I instinctively lowered my head, trying to block out the conversation. Arguments—*debates,* as Mother and Father called them—like this always erupted whenever they talked about work. My father wasn't one to cross when he got angry, especially if it was about the local Mages. I knew he wasn't mad at me, but the sound of his voice filled with anger was enough to count myself lucky I wasn't born a Mage.

"They think they know how to keep the peace!? Those flora-bloods know *nothing* about peace!"

"Calm down, honey! Can we for *once* not talk about the Mages? It's Erin's birthday, for Darwin's sake!"

As the argument—excuse me, *debate*—became more heated, their words piercing deep into my flesh like a million pins. Fear coursed through my veins like cold rapids. My heart pounded. My head spun. A rush of chemicals flowed through me. Raw emotion spread throughout my entire body. Everything was cold... *so cold...*

"Damn it, Evelyn!" Father shouted, abruptly stopping the debate. He rubbed his arms together. "Who adjusted the temperature? I thought we fixed the burner."

Mother mirrored him. "This is what we get for scavenging from construction sites, Tom," she replied venomously, still fuming over Father's outburst moments earlier. I didn't mind the change of subject even though they were still fighting.

Mother turned back towards me, her face gentler. "Stay in here and eat your cake, okay honey?" She asked, her quiet voice calm. A white cloud of warm air swirled out of her mouth as she exhaled. "Your father and I are going outside to fix the burner. We'll be back in a minute."

I nodded and stretched my arms. "Actually, I was going to go to bed," I replied, yawning deeply. "I'm tired. Can we put the cake in the refrigerator?"

Mother's eyebrows furrowed in worry. "Sure, honey," she replied after a moment's silence. A small smile appeared on her face. "Good night and happy birthday."

Father strode towards me, his eyes never once looking at me as Mother walked out the door towards the back of the house. "I'm sorry for getting upset with your mother on your birthday. I know how you feel about us de—I mean, fighting. Can you forgive me?"

I smiled and threw my arms around him. He was so tall that I had to jump to give him what I considered a good hug. "Of course, Father," I replied. "I love you."

"I love you too, honey." He squeezed me tightly before setting me on the floor. "Good night." He turned and walked out the rickety old door, shutting it firmly but softly behind him.

I stood there for a moment and sighed. I loved my family; but sometimes, I wished that the arguing and the fighting would end. One minute they would be all over each other, completely in love, and the next they would say such harsh things that one would never imagine that they could possibly be married. One sentence summed it up: their relationship was as bipolar as the ends of a magnet. But as all Chemists know, opposites attract.

I walked back to the kitchen and placed the half eaten cake in the refrigerator. We had saved enough for another night. I realized that I had never taken a slice of my own cake. I began to shut the door, but stopped. I opened the refrigerator back up and eyed the delectable dessert. I reached in and scooped a large portion of butter cream frosting with my finger and tasted it. The delicious flavor blocked everything but the sugar high. I took a deep breath as I felt a small rush of warmth run through me. *Yep, Mother once again got it right.*

A sudden wave of exhaustion hit me. As I turned around, my eyes fell to an entryway blocked by a dark red curtain, weathered from years of use. I dragged myself past the "door" and walked into a short hallway. On my left was my parent's bedroom, but that was not where I wanted to go. Instead, I took a sharp right. The room was dark, and I couldn't see a thing. I snapped my fingers, and the lights of my bedroom flashed on.

My room was small, but it was a safe haven from my parents' fighting. My room was also filled with things scavenged from construction sites like everything else in the house. A small bed was nestled against the back corner of the space. The path through the room was blocked by clothes and an assortment of items spilling from my closet. A long mirror served as the door to it. Opposite my bed was a dresser, where I kept more of my clothes. A display screen sat on top of it. Above my bed hung a red and black starred flag. Seven black stars formed a ring over a plain blood-red background. In the middle of the circle was a pair of gears. A nice metal desk and worktable completely stocked with Chemist equipment, a gift from my father's coworkers and the only really nice thing in the entire room, was below the only window, complete with a cushioned wooden chair.

I slowly moved towards my bed. The plush blankets were so inviting, and the very thought of burying myself in them only compounded my exhaustion. As I climbed into the bed, I laid down and pulled up the blankets until only my head was exposed. I brought my arm back out for only a moment to snap the lights off, and let the darkness of sleep take me.

I open my eyes and everything is white. There are no windows. I can't even distinguish between the walls and the floors.

"Hello?" I shout. My voice echoes in the white void. "Is anyone there?"

I start to run. I don't feel my feet landing on anything, but I can still hear a tapping noise on the floor. I feel like I could run forever. I keep running until I catch a glimpse of something in the corner of my vision. I turn around and see a strange golden anomaly, swirling in the air like liquid gold flowing in a current down a stream.

I should be afraid. I should run away. I should try to come up with a rational, scientific hypothesis for what I am seeing. At least, that is what my waking self would do. But instead, I find myself eerily calm. I don't know what it is, and for some reason I don't care. As the gold moves towards me, comforting warmth fills me inside. It moves closer and closer until it enters my body through my chest...

"Erin," a voice whispered. "Erin, honey, time to wake up."

I opened my eyes. Father hovered over me, fully dressed along with his lab coat. The room was still dark. I looked at the clock, its bright red letters shining into my eyes. *8:15 a.m.*

"Father?" I asked, still groggy.

"Get dressed," he replied. "We're going to the Lab."

CHAPTER TWO

I shook my head in an attempt to wake myself up.

"The Lab?" I asked, still confused. I rubbed my eyes. "Why am I going to the Lab?" I looked up to see Father in his favorite red pajama pants.

"No time for questions," he replied. "Someone very important is coming to the Lab today. I need you to be there." He tossed a white jacket identical to his onto the bed. "You need to wear this," he said. "Now hurry! We need to be there by 10:00!"

I gestured at the clock. "Why are we waking up so early, then?" I asked.

Dad threw his arms up. "Traffic is going to be a mess!" he replied. "Every Chemist in New Washington is coming today. Now get up!" He quickly left the room.

I sighed. Normally, those who were training to be Chemists did not begin in Labs until the age of twenty-five. I hadn't even reached the point in my training where I would go to the Lab to observe them. So why was Father so desperate to make me accompany him?

I gathered the lab coat in my arms and tossed my covers off of me. I snapped on the lights, but then winced as they blinded my tired eyes. I fell back on the bed. *This is so not happening today of all days!* I rolled myself out of bed and stumbled to my closet. *What am I going to wear? I don't even know who I'm meeting at the Lab or* silver cars rolled by, both on the road next to us, or about seventy-five feet above us. By now, the sun had risen, coloring the sky with shades purple and orange.

And it was there, in the sky, that I saw the epitome of New Pangaea's work.

The Gears.

The seven sprocket-like machines rotated slowly next to our moon, which was still visible in the early morning sky. But the great mechanism was only a quarter of the size of the moon, orbiting alongside it as they made their rotations around the Earth. A sense of awe and wonder filled me. Humankind had never before constructed something so large or fantastical. It was the result of years of planning and building on the part of the several governments of the Earth centuries ago.

It was also the very project that birthed New Pangaea.

"Look at them," my mother said, bringing me back to Earth and, more importantly, to the situation at hand. "Every morning when I wake up and head to the Lab, I look up and see *them*. They fill me with such hope for the future. They remind me of all the good work I do for New Pangaea." She turned to me. "It's also the same work that you will undertake in a few years."

"And for that, we are so proud of you," Father added.

Yeah, no pressure.

We walked over to our family's car. It was a ground vehicle, modeled after a car style from centuries ago—a station wagon. We drove a car which nearly made me the laughingstock of mine and my parents' peers. We were all about to pile into the vehicle when I heard a voice echoing from behind me.

"Good morning, Dr. Luciani!" a male voice called from across the street.

My father's attention shifted to the voice. A slim, young man about in his late twenties stood, smiling and waving at us. "Good morning, Damon!" he replied.

I followed my parents as they walked towards him. Unlike my hair, his golden locks were polished and clean, brushed into a professional style to where not one hair was out of place. His tanned skin was smooth and washed, free of any blemishes. I could tell that he had gotten corrective cosmetic surgery to get rid of his wrinkles. Damon was a... *unique* kind of Chemist, a member of the Security Division. While he wore a white lab coat identical to my parents', a silver security badge was displayed proudly on his chest, shining bright like the sun. Underneath the coat I could see the traces of a bright orange vest.

"I thought you would be at the Lab by now, Dr. Ritter, considering the special guest arriving today," my mother said.

Damon shook his head. "I'm on ground traffic control for now, ma'am," he replied. "Ground and air traffic have been heavy since the news spread. Let me tell you, I haven't seen New Washington this busy in a long time."

He turned to me, his plastic smile never reaching his eyes. "And good morning to you, Miss Erin," he said, holding out his hand.

I took his almost too firm handshake, wincing at its strength. He and my father were good friends, despite the age difference. Mother had known his family longer than I'd been alive.

"Good morning, Damon," I replied. His intense gaze seemed to burn my skin, making me more uncomfortable.

"That jacket looks a little big on you," he pointed out, a peculiar fire churning in his green eyes.

I could feel my face burning. I wrapped the coat around me, wanting to hide myself from his comments and his penetrating stare. I took a deep breath. *Easy, Erin. Calm down. Mother and Father are already stressed out as it is.*

"Sorry," I replied. "I'm borrowing one of my Father's spare ones."

He flashed me a vacant smile, as if he was staring at someone completely different. "I can fix it for you, if you'd like," he replied. I knew he meant well, but there was something about his tone...

"We actually have to go, Damon," Mother said. "We need to get Erin to the Lab."

Damon nodded his head. "I'm sorry, Mrs. Luciani," he said. "I completely lost track of time. Oh well, I guess I'll see both of you later. Goodbye." His gaze turned to me for an instant, that same intensity burning in his eyes, before turning away and return to traffic.

"What a nice young man," Father said, smiling at Damon. "An accomplished Chemist, and a polite one, too."

"Not to mention very handsome," Mother replied. She turned to me. "Who knows? Maybe you and Damon may find yourselves together one day," she added, checking the time. "Oh, Darwin! Honey," Mother exclaimed suddenly. "We're going to be late!" By now, the sun had risen further into the sky. The moon was barely visible, but I could still make out the outline of the Gears.

Father quickly pressed a button, and the doors of the vehicle opened. "We don't have much time," Mother said, her tone pushing us to move faster. She and Father quickly got into the car. I was surprised that I found it hard to keep up with their quick motions. Father started the car, pulled into the road, and sped towards the City.

CHAPTER THREE

We lived on the outskirts of New Washington. The homes were dilapidated, decorated with things scavenged from Construction sites. But the city was the fruition of our ancestors' dreams, a high-tech paradise. Tall silver skyscrapers towered over small houses where the poor lived, clouds churning around them. Flying cars soared above us. There was an unusual view of a sea of white coats. Every car, every bus, every pedestrian was converging into one building.

The New Washington Center for Scientific Studies, otherwise known as The Lab.

The short, stocky building was very wide and located in the center of the city while the skyscrapers surrounded it. Most of the work was completed in the main complex while some other divisions were located in adjacent buildings. Unlike the other places in town, this building was carved out of white quartz, modeled after an ancient structure from before the days of New Pangaea; I think it was called *The Capitol Building*. Normally, The Lab was a serious place, not really a place of celebration. But today was different. Thousands of Chemists flowed in and out of the doors. The streets were noisier. The beaming faces of the Chemists made the city seem brighter. A huge flag was hung from the roof, the blood red cloth providing a stark contrast to the shining rock. *Mineral,* my inner scientist corrected.

We'd been speeding along at a decent pace when I noticed that Father started to slow down considerably. "Damn it!" I heard him swear under his breath.

"What?" Mother asked concernedly as she placed a hand on his shoulder. As she turned her head to see what lay ahead of us, she froze. I started to ask what was wrong until I caught sight of them.

Mages. There must have been thousands of them. All were gathered in a large group in the streets, blocking the front of The Lab. Their faces were contorted with hatred, as their voices combined in a cacophony of anger. They were all blocked off by members of the Security Division for at least a mile. Their shouts were so loud I could hear them from inside the confines of the car.

"You are destroying our world!"

"Get out!"

"The Earth will have her revenge!"

As I glanced over the crowd, I began to notice how different the Mages all appeared. Some were tall and lanky like walking skeletons, while others could barely poke their heads above the crowd. Their skin was as dark as the night, or as pale as sheets. The one thing that seemed to unite them all was that each Mage had a series of vine-tattoos covering different parts of their bodies. Some had more tattoos than others. I didn't understand the significance of the number or the placement of these tattoos. I was about to turn away when a strange figure caught my eyes.

A young Mage was staring at me. A great, black robe cloaked most of her. I could barely see the tattoos inked across her face. A pair of icy blue eyes peered at me inquisitively. I was drawn to her cold gaze.

Father growled, bringing me back to reality. He squeezed the steering wheel; his knuckles turned white.

"Those damned flora-bloods." He stopped the car, and opened the door.

Mother grabbed his shirt sleeve. "Tom!" she shouted. "What are you doing!? Get back in the car! We need to get to The Lab!"

Father pulled away from her grasp. "Give me a minute, Evelyn," he said, the look in his eyes dangerous and downright frightening.

For a split second, everything was different.

The world seemed to stop. The rest of the world was grey, except for my father. His eyes were muddied red. The same color exuded from him like huge flames licking the air; I could practically feel their heat running across my skin.

I blinked. The world was back to normal. Father was shouting at a couple of Mages while Mother sat with me in the car, hanging her head down low to avoid being recognized. A couple of Security Chemists pulled him away. He sulked in defeat back to the car, shutting the door and refused to look at either of us.

"We need to go," he said as he started the car again. We moved slowly towards the giant quartz complex, an awkward silence seeming to consume everything.

"Tom," Mother said, breaking the stillness between us. "You know that He doesn't like it when we speak to them…"

"I know," Father replied. "I just… I wasn't thinking rationally. I let my emotions get the best of me. I… I just hate them. I…"

He fell silent as Mother ran her hand gingerly through his hair and smiled slightly at him. "It's okay, honey. Today is an important day, but it's also stressful."

Father nodded in agreement. He then turned to me. "I'm sorry for yelling, honey," he said. "Are you okay?" he asked. "I didn't scare you, did I?"

I didn't even notice that I was shaking furiously until he said something. I tried to slow down my rapid breathing. Everything around me was cold... The same cold that would fill the house whenever I felt any kind of negative emotion.

What's happening to me?

I shook my head, pretending nothing had happened. "Yeah, I'm fine," I said. "I'm just nervous, that's all."

Father's eyebrows furrowed. "Okay," he replied. He obviously didn't believe me. *Damn it.*

He looked at us as he stopped the car. "Are you ready?" he asked. Mother responded by wordlessly exiting the vehicle.

I took longer to get out. The cool breeze greeted me. The sky was gray and cloudy, as if all of the color in the city had vanished. I could feel cold water splash on my skin, slowly at first, then faster.

Father gestured towards the front door. "Quickly!" he shouted, running towards the large oak double doors. The rain poured down in buckets. It was like someone had opened a giant faucet over New Washington.

The doors opened automatically as we neared them. We ran inside, our lab coats dripping wet. Mother and Father tried to dry themselves off as quickly as they could.

But I remained motionless, awed by how massive the place was. The inside leagues more imposing than the outside. The ceilings towered above us. A grand glass rotunda was in the center of the lobby. I could see the gray sky and hear the rain beat against the rotunda. Along the massive main hall were doors that matched the front entrance. Most of the light was natural thanks to the glass structure, but there were still some smaller lamps hung along the perimeter in between each door. Forked paths stretched from the middle of the main hall; one to the left and one to the right. The walls were made of the same quartz as the outside. The floors were a shining grey and white marble, and I could see a distorted reflection of us in it. In the middle of the main hall, the seven stars seemed to spin in a circle on the floor, surrounding a pair of gears. The symbol of our country.

"We finally made it," Father said.

Mother looked up at the clock. "And not a moment too soon," she said, pointing at the time. *9:59 a.m.* A relieved laugh escaped Father's lips.

A strange thought occurred to me as I continued to look around the place. *Where was everyone?* I was about to ask my parents where all of the other Chemists were when I heard an odd noise.

"My goodness!" a strange voice said. "Are you all right!?"

Startled, my head snapped up. This may have been my first time in The Lab, but the voice didn't sound like it was from anywhere around New Washington. It was too... *formal.* I looked around, trying to find the source of the mysterious sound. I could hear footsteps echoing down the hall, but I couldn't locate the source. It wasn't until I saw a young man in his mid-twenties running down the hall toward us, his white lab coat flying in the wind behind him, that I was able to identify what—or rather, *who*—was the source.

"I heard what happened with the Mages," the man said, breathing heavily. His accent rang in my ears. "They are gathering all around the city; it is a mess out there."

Mother nodded, still shivering from the cold, wet rain. She immediately straightened up once her eyes met his. "Yes, we are fine, sir," she replied. I had never heard her address anyone like that, save for the few times I saw her with the Division Head.

Father did the same. "Yes, everything is fine," he echoed. He may have tried to appear like he was cool and collected, but I could see him shaking, his eyes darkening...

There it was again. A deep shade of purple radiated from his body. Only this time, it wasn't like a proud flame, but rather a dim light. I could read the colors around him. He was nervous, terrified even, of this stranger. But what was so special about this man that made Mother and Father so nervous?

I blinked. Once again the colors disappeared. I followed their eyes to the man's breast pocket. Two gears were embroidered on it. It was a symbol that I had never seen any Chemist in New Washington wear on their lab coat.

That's when I realized it. The special guest that Mother, Father, and everyone in New Washington was so anxious to meet.

This was him.

The young man took a bow. "Dr. Makswell Sharpe, lead scientist of the Golgotha Project, at your service."

CHAPTER FOUR

Wait. *The* Golgotha Project? The codename given to the project that was in charge of maintaining and protecting the Gears? No way!

I couldn't. I just couldn't wrap my head around it. *This* was the man who was in charge of the greatest project ever undertaken by mankind? His jet black hair, while neat and tidy, was long and pulled back into a pony tail which stretched down past his shoulders. His thin yet neatly trimmed goatee accented his smile. Chemists were required to cut their hair short above their shoulders, and to shave any facial hair.

Dr. Sharpe was a slob compared to other Chemists.

"I apologize for our tardiness, Dr. Sharpe," Father said, imitating his bow.

Dr. Sharpe shook his head. "No trouble at all," he replied, holding up his hand. "I completely understand. Those Mages can be quite a problem, can't they?" He chuckled.

The jab at Mages seemed to cause Father to relax a little. He even cracked a small smile. "Yes, sir, they can be." He held out his hand. "Dr. Thomas Luciani, Construction Division." Dr. Sharpe shook his hand. He gestured to Mother. "And this is my wife, Dr. Evelyn Luciani, Botany Division."

Mother held out her hand. "Pleasure to meet you, Dr. Sharpe," she said. But Dr. Sharpe gently kissed her hand.

"The pleasure—no, the *honor*—is all mine," he replied with a charming smile.

Both Mother's and Father's faces burned a bright red. I could feel Father's jealousy. An awkward silence filled the air, until Father broke it by clearing his throat.

He placed his hand on my shoulder. "And this is our daughter, Erin," he said, unintentionally squeezing my shoulder so hard I winced from the pain.

I bowed my head slightly to Dr. Sharpe, and held out my hand. I could feel sweat starting to form on my skin. "Pleased to meet you," I said, turning my gaze away from him as my voice cracked.

Dr. Sharpe grabbed my hand. I forced myself to look into his fierce sapphire blue eyes as they burned into mine. "The pleasure is mine, Erin," he replied, giving a small smile.

I should have been honored that he was allowing me to meet him, but the way he said my name sent chills down my spine. I couldn't figure out what it was about his tone that made me so uneasy, but I tried my best to push the thoughts out of my head.

"She's only twenty-one," Father continued, "so she isn't a Chemist yet, technically. But I thought this would be an excellent opportunity for her to learn about you and the Golgotha Project."

Dr. Sharpe smiled. "Of course," he replied. "Everything I will be discussing today is information that is open to the general public." He eyed the lab coat I was wearing. I could feel it practically falling off my shoulders. "Especially if that 'general public' is an aspiring Chemist." His attention returned to Mother and Father. "The other Chemists have already gathered in the auditorium. I can take you there, if you'd like."

Mother nodded. "That would be perfect, Dr. Sharpe," she said. "Again, we apologize--"

Dr. Sharpe held up his black gloved hand. Mother went silent. "I want no apologies," he replied. Father winced as his commanding voice boomed throughout the hall. "I just want you to enjoy the presentation. Follow me, please." He turned and led us down the hall. At the end of the hall was a set of maple wood doors guarded by two Security Chemists.

Dr. Sharpe stopped and turned to us. "Go ahead and enter," he said. "I will take another way in. Walking in with you would cause too much chaos." The Security Chemists eyed us, imposing and threatening in their black uniforms despite the fact that they wore white lab coats over their clothes just like us.

"Marcus, Jackson," he said, obviously completely comfortable using their first names. "Let them enter. The Mages blocked their way to The Lab; that is why they were late." The two Security Chemists bowed their heads and stepped aside.

Dr. Sharpe took a left towards another, more obscure maple wood door. "I hope you enjoy the conference," he said as he stepped through the door.

"Such a lovely gentleman," Mother sighed longingly as she touched the hand he kissed.

Father rolled his eyes. "He's okay," he replied. "We'll just have to wait and see how impressive he is."

Yes, I thought. *Yes, indeed.*

The two great doors opened, revealing a spacious auditorium. There were three different levels of chairs surrounding the center stage, counting the ground floor we had entered. The walls were draped with maroon curtains, which matched the chairs in the room. Bright lights were scattered around the room. I could hear the scraping and shuffling of my boots as we hastened our way across the rough black carpet. In the center of the hall was a large stage, consisting of a podium and a table with a model of the Gears. Projector screens hung to the left and right of it. New Pangaea's flag was suspended above the stage. The seats were already almost filled; it was a daunting task to find one empty seat, let alone three.

"We may have to sit apart," Mother said worriedly, looking desperately around the room to find vacant seats.

I was ready to turn back and wait in the car, until I heard that familiar voice from earlier this morning.

"Well, if it isn't the Lucianis!" Damon's voice pierced through the noisy crowd. I turned to see him waving at us to get our attention. Mother and Father walked towards him briskly while I lagged behind.

"Good to see you again, Damon," Father said, reaching out to shake his hand, which Damon shook earnestly.

"How did you get here before us?" Mother asked. "I thought you would still be directing traffic."

"Funny story," Damon laughed. "Just after you left, my replacement arrived. So, I decided to come here; I've always been fascinated with the Golgotha Project."

"Why aren't you outside helping to stop the protestors?" I inquired.

Damon turned to me, narrowing his eyes. "I may be older than you, but I've only been working in the Security Division for a short time. Only those who are veterans are out there today." He stood up and gestured towards three empty chairs next to him. "Three Chemists are outside working security and traffic. They said they wouldn't be back for the conference. Would you like to have their seats?"

Mother smiled, putting a hand to her chest. "Why, we would be honored." She turned to me. "Wouldn't we, Erin?" she asked.

I swallowed. "Sure."

"Excellent," Damon replied, smiling. He stepped out of the row, making a path toward the empty seats. "Have a seat."

Mother and Father walked past me into the seats, leaving one empty chair right next to Damon.

"You can sit down," Damon chuckled. But there was something about his laugh, something that didn't feel right. *Is it the tone? No...* "I won't bite."

Part of me didn't believe him, but as my parents eyed me inquisitively, coaching me to sit down, I sighed and shimmied into the aisle of chairs. But as I passed by him, my body froze.

His hands rested on my hips, guiding me to the empty seat. But he stopped me momentarily and breathed deeply in delight as my body rested on his front. I could feel a hard bulge pressing into my backside. I shut my eyes, praying for Mother, Father, just *someone* to say something...

Damon gently pushed my hips aside, allowing me to sit down. My blood ran cold; all of my senses were blocked. The temperature around me seemed to fall more and more every second. I took several deep breaths, trying to calm myself. I turned to Mother and Father. Neither of them had noticed what Damon had just done; they sat facing each other, carrying on a conversation as if the rest of the world didn't exist.

"I'm glad you're here," Damon whispered, leaning closer to me. "This man is incredibly intelligent; you'll definitely learn a lot today."

I shivered, biting my lip to hold back my tears of humiliation. *I think I've learned more today than I've ever wanted to know.*

The lights dimmed, causing the voices of the Chemists to drop as well. A single spotlight was aimed at the stage. At this point, the entire auditorium was filled with an almost deafening silence. A fluttering flag was shown on the projection screens, accompanied by the loud, triumphant sound of New Pangaea's anthem. The room filled with the sound of people rising in reverence to their global nation. I stood up with everyone in my row, but felt the music slower than before, as I felt Damon's cold hand around my hip.

A much cheerier musical track faded in over the speakers, growing louder and louder as an announcer's voice cried, "Ladies and gentlemen, the lead scientist of the Golgotha Project in London, Dr. Makswell Sharpe!"

The applause and cheers were deafening. The music exploded as Dr. Sharpe walked out to the front of the stage, waving at everyone. But he didn't seem fazed at all by their praise, remaining humble even in his greeting. He walked to the podium and pulled out a small, sleek tablet from his side coat pocket.

Even though the music diminished, the applause remained. Dr. Sharpe modestly bowed his head, which only fueled the audience's fervor. As he held up his black gloved hands, the room grew silent, eagerly awaiting his first word.

"My fellow Chemists," his voice rang throughout the room. "It is an honor to be here this morning. I remember the days when I was like you, working in London's Laboratory Center for Science. I was once a member of the Computer Division. I spent day and night in that place, working to make life better for my fellow citizens, often to the chagrin of the city's Mages." A collective, quiet sound of disgust echoed in the hall.

"But regardless," he continued, "I did everything I could to make not only London, but New Pangaea a safe place for all. And it was my revolutionary work in supercomputer engineering that landed me a job as the lead scientist on the Golgotha Project.

"New Pangaea's history is known by all citizens. One thousand years ago, our ancestors laid aside their differences in order to save a broken world. World War Three had ravaged the planet, destroying much of the Earth's natural resources. In order to save the human race, all of the nations of the world combined their resources to create the Gears, large machines that would orbit the Earth alongside our Moon, and would provide job security and power for the world.

"The newfound global nation of New Pangaea was born.

"Each of the seven continents offered to build two Gears: one to send into orbit, and one to keep on Earth. The Gears created jobs and united mankind. Crime and poverty rates dropped to an all-time low. There was no war. The newly named 'Golgotha' Project brought about the most peaceful period in human history.

"Alongside this scientific revolution, a new class arose: Mages—those who had the ability to practice and control magic. The Mages asked for peace amongst the Chemists, offering their services to the glory of New Pangaea. The eons-old conflict between science and magic seemed to have been resolved.

"But not every Mage believed in the vision of the Golgotha Project, and shortly after the founding of New Pangaea, a group of radical Mages attempted a *coup d'état* and seized control of the Mages' society...."

"The Mages have done everything to stop progress ever since!" a rogue voice echoed from the audience.

"No, no," Dr. Sharpe replied, shaking his head. "That—"

The entire audience erupted in a wave of boos and hisses. But they weren't for Dr. Sharpe. No, they were for the Mages. He brought his hands up, attempting to calm the crowd, but the noise just kept getting louder and louder. Mother, Father and even Damon joined in with the crowd.

"Those damned flora-bloods!"

"They know nothing of human progress!"

I should have done so, too. I should have felt a violent hatred for the Mages, just as all the other Chemists did. I should have joined in the screams and cries of outrage and hurt. I should have felt hot fire burning through me.

But all I felt was the grip an icy chill. Goosebumps began to form on my arms. *What should I do?* I looked up at Dr. Sharpe, half expecting him to have given up and joined in the throng, screaming at the very existence of Mages.

He wasn't. His face was buried in his hands. I could feel the guilt and shame radiate from him as he stood there, silent and unmoving.

"We should go out there and show those damned... *things* what happens when they mess with human progress!" the first voice snarled.

The audience roared in agreement. Every Chemist in the audience was heading for the doors, each one anxious to get out and express their righteous anger. Mother and Father pushed past me, their faces bright red and contorted with rage.

As the auditorium emptied and the last echoes of the crowd faded away, I looked back up at Dr. Sharpe. His expression was the same as mine – sad and fearful.

"Dear God," he muttered. "We are in trouble."

CHAPTER FIVE

It was less than a minute before the entire auditorium emptied except for Dr. Sharpe and myself. The tiniest noise echoed loudly.

I looked up at the doctor. He hurriedly packed up what little he had, jumped off the stage and ran. The same haunted, fearful expression was still on his face.

I had no idea what to do. I wasn't angry at anyone, and I couldn't understand why everyone else was. I couldn't fathom why any Chemist would think that starting a riot was a good idea. Going outside and fighting the resident Mages would cause more harm than good. What if they questioned my loyalty to the Chemists? No Lab would want someone who didn't stand up for the good of New Pangaea.

But that was just the thing. Fighting *wouldn't* be for the good of New Pangaea. Wasn't the point of New Pangaea to unite as one? This wasn't how you unite people. From watching Dr. Sharpe speak, I knew that I wasn't alone in my beliefs, especially after I saw his reaction to the raging crowd.

"Doctor!" I cried, walking briskly after him. "Dr. Sharpe!"

He turned around, his ponytail waving in the breeze. "Miss Erin," he said, surprised. "What is it? I do not have much time. It is utter chaos out there."

I opened my mouth, but my mind went completely blank. I couldn't say a word to the man. "Uh... um..." I stuttered.

"Look, I cannot answer questions or give comments right now," he said. "I need to correct this mistake." He turned around and started to walk away.

I grabbed his sleeve, stopping him in his tracks. He turned back to me, glaring.

I took a deep breath, unconsciously trying to avoid the intensity of his gaze. "I want to help you."

Dr. Sharpe froze, taken aback by my comment. "Come again?" he asked, surprised.

"I want to help you," I replied. "I don't want to fight. I've never been a fighter. I... I'd rather stay behind and help you."

Dr. Sharpe completely turned around to face me. "I am not staying behind," he said, his voice strong and forceful. "Someone needs to go out there and stop this."

My stomach dropped. The same ice that had enveloped me earlier was back, colder than ever. I tried as hard as I could to stand straight and proud in front of such an important man, working hard to mask my anxiety.

Dr. Sharpe sighed. He took my hand and guided me out the door. I followed him as he took a sharp left.

This hall was just as grand as the rest of the place. Giant crystal chandeliers hung from the high, rounded ceilings. Paintings of great scientists lined the quartz walls. It was almost like a palace.

The two of us hurried down the corridor until we reached a wooden door secured with a small silver lock. Everything about the entrance screamed that we shouldn't be there.

I looked up at Dr. Sharpe. "Um, Doctor..."

Dr. Sharpe kicked open the door before I could say anything else.

My jaw dropped. "D-Doctor Sharpe!" my voice barely a whisper, in fear of getting caught. "What the hell are you—?"

"Upstairs is a vacant laboratory," he offered. "If you wish to stay inside away from the fight, you will be able to stay up there. Do not worry about getting caught. No one has been in this laboratory in years. Once you are ready to leave, go back down these steps."

I looked at him. "Where are you going to go?" I asked.

He looked down the hall, refusing to make eye contact with me. "Someone has to go out there," he replied. "Earth cannot afford another war." Still refusing to look at me, he took off down the hall.

I slowly turned to the staircase. It extended upwards through a shadowy corridor. Cobwebs lined the wall, the floor dusty and weathered. My heart pounded loudly in my ears as I stared into the blackness, but I was willing to take any chance that was offered to me to avoid fighting. I started to climb up the steps when I heard a voice from down the hall.

"Wait, Miss Erin!" Dr. Sharpe's voice echoed through the hall.

I turned my head, and saw Dr. Sharpe's head poke around the corner of the hallway, his eyes piercing yet gentle. A small smile ran across his face.

"You are wise, Miss Erin," he said simply. "Wise beyond your years." He then vanished. His footsteps echoed and grew quiet.

Wise? I wondered as I ascended the dismal staircase. *Running away from a fight is not wise in the least bit.*

My coughs reverberated up and down the dusty corridor. *Damn,* I thought. *It's not even this bad at home.*

The stairs seemed to stretch for an eternity. After what felt like hours of climbing, I came across a metal door. The iron was splattered with red rust that stained the door like aged, dried blood. But a small ray of light shone through a crack in the door. I narrowed my eyes. *I wonder...* I walked up to the entrance, pressed my body against the cold metal, and pushed as hard as I could. The ancient door scraped against the floor, the noise ringing in my ears.

I stopped, unable to take much more, and looked at the progress I had made. The door had barely moved, but it was enough for me to squeeze my tiny frame through.

My eyes widened as I moved through the crack into the room. It was an old laboratory, one that for some reason had been shut away from the rest of The Lab. But what kind of laboratory was it? Metal tables lined the room, complete with weathered metal stools and dusty beaker sets. The walls were yellowed with age, the floors caked with old dirt and mud. The only light came from large windows on the other side of the room, though it was dimmed and clouded by the years of built up dust.

It looked like any other laboratory. But why was this one abandoned?

At this point, I didn't care why. I just wanted to be out of the way of the fight. There were plenty of places to hide. There was barely enough room under the tables for me to duck under them. In the event someone figured out I had found their abandoned laboratory, I could move the chairs around, allowing me to hide better. There were huge closets in the corners of the room probably used to store equipment. Certainly, they were large enough to fit someone my size.

As I scoped out the room for other hiding spots I could hear loud screams and cries from outside. The noise grew louder as I walked towards the windows. I rolled up the sleeves of my lab coat, wiped the windows and looked below.

The fight. I was right above the fight.

From my point of view, I was about two or three stories above the confrontation. The Chemists and Mages were screaming at each other, faces contorted with rage. Several of the Chemists had run into the opposing mob and begun beating the Mages. I scanned the rest of the crowd. Women and children began to fight as well. Wives and mothers tried futilely to hold back their husbands and sons. But the men would have none of it. They pulled themselves free of their grasps. The tearful screams of the women blended into the angry cacophony. Blood flooded the streets.

Burning fire coursed through my veins. This wasn't helping New Pangaea! All this talk of progress, but to what avail? What is the first thing we do when we get angry? We beat the ones who are different until they can no longer stand.

My eyes focused on a familiar hooded figure in the crowd of Mages as I surveyed the carnage. I had seen this Mage on the way to the conference this morning. The girl lifted her hood and removed the robe, allowing it to fall onto the bloody pavement. She appeared to be about my age. Her platinum blonde hair cascaded past her shoulders. She just stood there watching the riot taking place. A navy floor-length gown wrapped around her small, fragile body. Her pale skin shone. She was unlike anyone I had ever seen. I gasped as her gaze lifted upwards, the fire that had been burning within me freezing dead in its tracks.

She was staring right at me.

How did she—how *could* she—know that I was up here? Dr. Sharpe had assured me that no one used this room or even knew about it. *Dr. Sharpe!* Maybe she knew him! That would mean that Dr. Sharpe was conspiring with Mages! He wasn't from here; he had spent his life growing up in London. Regardless, she was here. She knew I was up here. I wanted to talk to her, ask her questions. Who was she? How did she know who I was? I didn't care if it meant going down into the fray. I needed answers.

The woman's gaze turned sharply from me as I continued to watch the battle and contemplated going down into the brawl. I spotted a rogue Chemist as I followed her eyes. The Chemist was running towards the Mage with something in his hand. I tried to get a better view, but all I could see was a red liquid swishing around inside the hollow handle of a dagger.

My stomach dropped. Arsenoformic acid. The most dangerous chemical in New Pangaea.

I banged my hands against the window. I tried to get her attention. Tried to warn her. I screamed. I pounded more. She couldn't hear me over the deafening violence occurring below. I stared at her, tears welling at my eyes. I knew that she wasn't going to make it, and she knew it as well. Yet she calmly stayed put, as if the Chemist didn't exist.

She slowly turned back to me, her eyes filled with sadness. The Chemist drew near. I don't know how it was possible, but I could clearly see her mouth a message to me.

"Be not afraid."

The dagger pierced her heart. She was dead before she hit the ground.

The fire that was frozen in me now raged hotter than ever. She was innocent! She had no part in this fight! How could he!? My head swam, dizzy with shock. I couldn't take it anymore. I kept my eyes focused on the Chemist that had murdered the girl. He trotted victoriously back to his friends, where they gloated in his kill. The Mages stopped fighting and stared at the girl's corpse, frozen in grief, as if they knew her. Disgust only fueled my anger. The heat that had encompassed my whole body traveled through me to my left hand. It grew hotter; it was on fire. By instinct, I outstretched and stretched open my hand. The heat immediately left it.

The ground beneath the cheering Chemists exploded.

It was as if someone had triggered mines under them. Their bodies flew backwards, rocked by the strains of the blast. They landed in awkward positions on the road. The fight immediately stopped. The attention of every person turned towards the Chemists. The other Chemists looked terrified, unable to use science to deduce what had just happened. The Mages, on the other hand, appeared merely confused. What—or who—caused this? They were unable to figure out where it had originated.

Cold fear gripped me. I looked down at my hand. It was pink and hot, like a mild burn.

It was me. *I* did it.

I used magic.

CHAPTER SIX

No. No! That was impossible. I couldn't have used magic! I'm a *Chemist*—well, Chemist in training, but close enough. Chemists don't use magic. We rely on real world observation and what we can create with our hands. As I looked down at my palms, I grew dizzy, not from rage, but from exhaustion and fear. Whatever just occurred could not be explained by science.

What was happening to me? What would I tell Mother? Father? They would never forgive me. And The Lab. I'd never get a placement now. Who would want a Chemist who practiced magic on her own people? Questions and fears raced around my head. I began to hyperventilate, no longer worried about hiding at this point.

There was only one thing my body could do at this point. *Run.*

I broke into a frantic sprint, desperately trying to move through the crack in the doorway as quickly as possible. *I have to get out of here!*

I could feel a searing pain in my hand. I moved the slightly torn sleeve. I noticed that not only my hand, but my arm down about halfway to my elbow was pink. I winced as the stinging sensation lanced through it. *A first degree burn?* My inner scientist thought. *How did I get burns from magic?* I shook my head. *No, no. I have to stop thinking about this.* I hid my hands in my pockets. I figured I would put some dermis cream on it when I got home.

I descended the cold, dark staircase. The bright lights of The Lab welcomed me. I turned around and studied the door. The old wood showed signs of damage. I couldn't let the other Chemists find out I had been up there. Maybe... maybe I could use my magic to fix it... just this once... just to cover my tracks... and then I would never use it again...

I shook my head, trying to shove the thoughts out of my head. *No, I couldn't use magic! What if someone saw?* I looked around. Everyone was still outside cleaning up the mess I had made. Still, I didn't want to risk getting caught. Darwin only knows the kind of advanced surveillance they have here.

I sighed. The same heat that flowed through me earlier ran through my arm and down my fingers as I pulled the door shut. A dim, gold light radiated from my hand. As I gripped the door handle, all evidence that the door had been damaged vanished. It was as if I had never been there in the first place.

Panicking again, I withdrew my hand. *No, no, no, no! Not again!* I ran down the hall. *Which way do I go?* My desperation had me confused, lost in my paranoia. *Left? Right? Left? I don't know!* I just kept running and running, hoping to escape the magic.

I arrived at the first intersection of halls in the front of The Lab. Relief and dread washed over me as I saw the great maple wood doors. I just wanted to go home... but what if someone saw me? The faces on the Mages... it was as if they had seen it before. What if someone saw me in the window?

I took a deep breath. I knew what I had to do.

I pushed open the great doors and walked outside. The smell of freshly fallen rain and blood assaulted my senses. I stuck my hands in the giant pockets of my lab coat again, hoping to hide the burns. The streets were still echoed with the hushed, concerned voices of both the Mages and Chemists tending to their wounded. I couldn't see anyone tending to the hooded woman. I looked around the crowd of Chemists, hoping to find Mother and Father. I just wanted to go home.

"Erin!" Mother called to me. I turned and smiled when I saw my parents hurrying to me as quickly as they could.

Mother wrapped her arms around me tightly. "Oh, dear, I am so sorry," she said, fighting back tears. "We were so worried about you."

"We thought you had run out with the rest of us," Father continued, running his fingers through my hair. "We thought you were with Damon when we didn't see you. We found him, but not you. He said that he hadn't seen you since the conference. We dropped everything to look for you."

"We thought the worst when those explosives went off," Mother said, burying her face in my shoulder.

I looked at them, tears welling in my eyes. "Can we just go home?"

Mother released me and nodded. "Yes, that sounds wonderful." She turned to Father. "What do you think, dear?"

Father nodded. "I think that is perfect." We walked past the crowds towards our vehicle. For once, the sight of that station wagon comforted me, and I could see why Father loved it so.

"I'll fix you some cabbage and bean stew when we get home," Mother said while rubbing my back. We climbed into the car and proceeded to drive slowly back to our house.

That was when I saw them. Strange, pale men and women with dark hair and their black coats flowing in the wind. Their eyes were replaced with what appeared to be black robotic lenses. Their pale lips pursed into a thin line as if they didn't have mouths.

The Silent Ones.

I had never seen them before. Their motivation was unknown, and generally the talk of conspiracy theories. Some believed that they were the secret agency that answered directly to the Supreme Leader Himself. Others believed that they were an underground arm of the Security Division. They say that one only sees them in times of great danger, such as when the security of New Pangaea itself is being threatened. Just their appearance was enough to scare one into giving them any secret they wanted. I stood there, frozen, watching them as they glided through the square, their eyes scanning their surroundings. Whatever they were, they definitely weren't human.

But why would the Silent Ones be called in because of a riot? Was it because of Dr. Sharpe?

Dr. Sharpe. Where did he go? What happened to him after he left me at the entrance to that old lab?

These questions echoed in my mind on the ride home, and for the rest of the afternoon. By dinner, I didn't even want to leave my bedroom. I just wanted to lay bed, but I also didn't want to be left alone with my thoughts. *What if the Silent Ones saw my magic and are coming for me?* I should have just gone out with my parents and Damon like a normal Chemist would. Then this would have never happened. Why couldn't I just have the courage to fight with the others?

A soft knock at my door brought my focus back to the real world. "Erin?" Mother whispered. I sat up and turned to her, snapping on the lights.

Mother took this as an invitation. She came in carrying a metal tray with a steaming bowl of soup and a slice of bread.

"Is everything all right, dear?" she asked as she set the tray on the desk next to my bed. She took a seat next to me. "You have been very quiet ever since we came home." I refused to make eye contact with her, causing her to become more concerned. "Honey, I am so sorry for this afternoon," she continued, putting an arm around me. "I should have made sure you were okay. Your father and I just wanted to look our best in front of Dr. Sharpe."

"I know," I replied, resting my head on her shoulder. "I just feel like I'm not a good Chemist because I didn't go out there with you."

"Oh, sweetie," she said, running her fingers gently through my hair. "Frankly, I am glad you were not out there. It would have torn your father and I apart if you had been hurt. The Security Division reported at least five people had been killed, four of them Chemists, in a mysterious explosion outside The Lab."

My stomach lurched. My blood ran cold. *Oh, no.*

"The Security Division says that the source of the explosion is still unknown," Mother continued. "But I am willing to bet that it was the Mages. Who else could have triggered something like that without chemicals, and without leaving a residue on the bodies?"

I refused to look at Mother. This had to be a nightmare. My uncontrolled magic killed them.

No! I shoved the thoughts of magic out of my head. That wasn't magic. Maybe it was just a coincidence. Maybe it was a different Mage. Or maybe it wasn't magic at all. I hoped it wasn't.

Mother kissed my head. "I'm just glad you're safe," she said. "Although how you avoided the fight is beyond me."

I shrugged. I laid my head in silence against Mother's shoulder. We heard a knock at my door. Mother's attention shifted to Father, his face pale and frozen in surprise.

"Is everything alright, dear?" Mother asked, concerned.

Father's eyes turned to me, wide with shock. "Someone is at the door for you, Erin," he replied. "Go greet our guest."

I felt like I was going to throw up. *It's over. It's all over.* I slowly walked past Father. They followed. I had no idea how I was able to walk with my legs feeling like gelatin. I pushed open the curtain and walked through the kitchen to the living room. Whoever was at the door had already invited themselves into the house. I stopped. Fear was slowly replaced with confusion.

Dr. Sharpe was sitting on the sofa, along with Marcus and Jackson.

He stood and greeted me with a smile and a bow. "A pleasure to see you again, Miss Erin," he said.

I raised an eyebrow. "Hello," I replied. I mentally kicked myself. *Really? That's the best I can say?* I shook my head. "Why are you here?" I asked.

Dr. Sharpe smiled. "Finding your address was easy," he answered with a chuckle. "Your family is the only one in New Washington with a station wagon." He gestured to the sofa facing him. "Why don't you have a seat? I have something very important I would like to discuss." I walked over to the chair and sat down.

"Would you like some lunch, Dr. Sharpe?" Mother asked.

Dr. Sharpe bowed his head. "No, thank you, Mrs. Luciani," he replied. "I will not take long." His attention shifted to me.

"The New Washington Center for Scientific Studies has been monitoring your progress in your studies, Miss Erin," he began. "You have been doing very well in all fields of science, especially in engineering, physics and astronomy. Your professors have praised your performance throughout your education, and claim that regardless of the field you are assigned to, you will be a blessing for all of New Pangaea.

"I will admit, this tour of sorts I have been taking through New Pangaea has been... selfish in nature. I have been giving talks throughout the world to not only see the future of New Pangaea's Chemists, but to find a new member for the Golgotha Project. It is not enough that one excels in science, but they also must be able to control themselves. I told you today that you were wise beyond your years. You showed great wisdom not giving into rage. You were wise by refusing to become violent. You have proven that you do not let prejudice cloud your judgment.

"The Golgotha Project needs new blood, Miss Erin. And that new blood is *you.*"

My jaw dropped.

"B-but is that even possible?" Father interjected. "She hasn't finished her studies yet!"

Dr. Sharpe nodded. "Yes, that is true," he replied. "But exceptions have been made before. She will come with me to London and complete her training. However, with this program, she will be able to become a certified Chemist before the age of twenty-three." His gaze fixed on me. "That is, if she so chooses. This must be your decision, Miss Erin."

I had no idea what to think. So many thoughts ran through my head. To go to London... to become part of the work that birthed New Pangaea. It would be the greatest career move I ever made. I could immerse myself in science, and I could make a difference for New Pangaea. I could start over and pretend that the magic incident never happened.

No, no, I corrected myself. *It wasn't magic. It was just a coincidence.*

"I understand that this is a big decision for you to make," Dr. Sharpe said, interrupting my thoughts. "I also understand that you may need time to consider this, though I do hope you take me up on my offer. As part of the Golgotha Project, you would live in the apartments in London saved specifically for Golgotha Chemists. Your training would consist of hands-on work with members of the project. This is a rare opportunity; we haven't had a new addition in many years. But like I said, think it over. I have a few last minute errands to run, as well as oversee the riot clean-up. I will not be leaving for London immediately. Meet me at Terminal 4B at the New Washington Airport at 7:30 pm in two days if you wish to accept my offer. Should you feel inclined to reject it, do not bother to come and we will not speak again." He stood up and gestured for his bodyguards to do the same. He walked to the door. Marcus opened it. He turned and gave one last bow.

"I hope to see you soon, Miss Erin." And like that he was gone.

CHAPTER SEVEN

Silence filled the house. My jaw was still on the floor. I couldn't believe any of what had just happened.
He had just invited me to be part of the most prestigious program in the world.

"Ahh!" Mother's squeals of delight rang through the house. She wrapped her arms around me. Father placed a hand on my shoulder. "Well done, Erin," he said.

I shrugged my shoulders, still in shock. "Well, that was unexpected," I replied.

"Unexpected, but wonderful!" Mother cried, kissing my head.

I had never seen my parents so happy. Pride swelled within them, their energy contagious. I always thought I would spend my life as an average Chemist: assigned to a particular field of study, lucky to even be able to move to a nicer part of New Washington. I assumed my life was here. But with the Golgotha Project, so many new doors were opened for me. I may have been driven by fear today, but for the first time in what felt like an eternity, I was in charge of my destiny. Infectious adrenaline ran through me. A gentle breeze blew behind me, but then it grew faster, faster. Objects began falling off of their shelves. The flag which hung on the wall fluttered violently and eventually flew off.

And then all of a sudden, the winds died down, leaving behind only silence.

Mother looked around, her hair flowing in all directions. "What's going on, honey?" she asked, brushing the hair from her face. "Did you leave the window open again?"

Father groaned. "I am not sure, but we can go check." He turned to me. "I am sorry, Erin," he said.

I shook my head. "It's alright," I replied.

"I swear, you can be so forgetful..." Mother mumbled as she walked to the back of the house. Father followed close behind her.

I became confused as I watched them leave. I could feel how strong the breeze was, as if a tornado had torn right through the house. I thought about how the weather was outside today. While it had rained, there was almost no breeze. I stood up, walked to the door, and opened it. The gray clouds remained, but small rays of sunshine began to poke through them like beacons of hope. I stepped outside and spread my arms, waiting to feel the wind run through my hair. I waited and waited... but not even a gentle breeze brushed against my skin.

I walked back inside. Where could that breeze have come from? Perhaps it was an isolated incident? *No,* I thought. The wind was too strong; there would have had to be some kind of tornado or severe weather outside. Cloudy isn't exactly a worst case scenario. I ran my fingers through my hair, trying to think of a rational explanation for the winds that almost destroyed our living room.

But after everything that happened today, what if...

What if it was magic?

I held my head in my hands as I tried to push the thoughts out of my mind. *I'm going crazy...* And yet, was I? I couldn't remember the last time our burners actually worked properly. They always broke whenever I was in the throes of panic, or mania, or sadness. After today, I had so many questions and no answers. I couldn't get the answers I wanted—or needed—if I stayed in New Washington.

I had to go to London.

******

The next two days were a blur. Most of the time was spent either sorting out paperwork to leave school or working the cleanup in the City. What little time I had to myself I spent packing my things. I had no time to relax or process what was happening. All of New Washington became caught up in the excitement when they heard that I was selected for the Golgotha Project. I saw my face everywhere: signs and broadcasts flashing in the night sky. Strangers would come up to me to shake my hand and congratulate me. I had gone from a sheltered Chemist-in-training to a local celebrity overnight.

People followed our family station wagon all the way to the airport that evening. Everyone insisted on coming to the airport to say goodbye. This newfound, albeit short-lived, fame didn't help ease the claustrophobia washing over me. I sighed in relief as staff members pushed the crowds away.

I only carried a small bag filled with clothes and a few personal items. "Everything you obtain in London will be brand new," Mother had insisted. Part of me knew she was right. But I still wanted to wear *my* gold headband, and sleep in *my* blankets at night. I wanted a piece of home.

The staff members led us down a hallway, past the terminals that many airships used. My eyebrows furrowed. "Why are we passing the terminals, sir?" I asked one of the staff members.

He turned to me, staring at me quizzically with his hazel eyes. "I thought you knew," he replied. "Dr. Sharpe has his own private terminal."

A private terminal? I thought as we stopped in front of a set of metal doors. *Why would he need a private terminal?* My eyes widened as the staff members opened the doors to the terminal. I could *definitely* see why.

The ceilings were several stories high, held up by posts which seemed to stretch for miles. Red and yellow lights flashed around the gray, metallic room. A cool breeze blew through my hair, making it gently move over my shoulders. The reds, yellows, and pinks of the sunset lit up the terminal as the sun's last light shone through the open entrance—or exit, as it was tonight. The largest airship I had ever seen faced the exit.

The bronze, almost gold, machine stood out against the grayness of the place. Specks of silver were scattered over the body of the ship. I could see its wings folded into itself, like a great bird waiting to take flight. *It's even bigger than this!?* Crew members dressed in gray bustled in and out of the airship's doors carrying supplies and tools. I could feel myself shrinking, becoming nothing more than a bacterium in the moving organism of the terminal. I searched the room, trying to find one thing that would be familiar to me.

The crew members continued to work, oblivious of us. I could see Dr. Sharpe, clad in that same lab coat I first saw him in, standing at the entrance to the airship. Next to him was a tall man in a white military uniform whom I presumed to be the captain. His grizzled face could have intimidated even the bravest of people, though Dr. Sharpe just stood there unfazed as they spoke. If anything, the captain seemed to be intimidated by him. Dr. Sharpe's gaze turned to me. He shook the captain's hand, patted him on the shoulder, and walked towards me.

"Miss Erin," Dr. Sharpe said, holding out his hand. I took it, unable to shake the weird feeling I got whenever he would say my name. His iron grip made pain shoot up through my hand. "A pleasure to see you again. We will be ready to leave shortly." He released my hand and turned to my parents. "I trust that everything is in order?"

Father nodded. "Yes, sir," he replied. "Erin has her forms from school in her bag."

Dr. Sharpe nodded. "And you have no qualms about your daughter leaving?" he added with a smile.

Mother shook her head. "We know that this is an amazing opportunity for her," she responded. "We will miss her dearly, but we know that she will become a great Chemist."

Dr. Sharpe clapped his hands together. "Excellent!" he said. He turned back to me. "We will depart momentarily, Miss Erin. The captain is attending to some last minute inspections. I will see you on board."

As he walked away, I looked at Father and Mother. They smiled at me, trying to hold themselves together. Their red eyes betrayed their emotions. My heart broke. I dropped my bag and ran into their arms. I could stay in my parents' embrace forever. I never had anyone other than my family, and now I was leaving them. I wanted to go back in time and pretend none of this ever happened. But I knew *that* life had come to an end.

"You are such a smart, strong, beautiful woman," Mother said, choking back tears. I rested my head on her shoulder, committing every detail to my memory: her hair, her smile that always showed off her teeth, the way she always smelled of lilacs and peppermint. "You always have been, and you always will be."

"Our only regret is that we weren't better parents," Father added, his voice shaking. His tears landed on my shirt, his embrace holding me closely. I could feel his body rock to the rhythm of his sobs.

I shook my head, my face wet with my own sweat and tears. "Are you crazy?" I asked. I buried my face into Father's lab coat, worn down and rough from years of work. "You are the greatest parents anyone could ask for. I wish I could stay here with you and have things be the way they always were."

Mother wiped away my tears with her thumb. "Every Chemist must begin her journey alone," she said. "I just never dreamed that it would be this soon." She cleared her throat. "Now, Erin. Before you go, your father and I have some words of wisdom for you."

"And gifts," Father added.

Mother rolled her eyes. "Question everything. If you do not know an answer or are not satisfied with the one you are given, seek it out."

"Science is the process of discovery," Father continued, "and this process never ends. One thing ends and another just begins."

Mother reached into a bag. She pulled out a folded white cloth and handed it to me. As I unfolded it, I felt hot tears once again welling in my eyes.

A lab coat.

The familiar design comforted me. I was struck most by the emblem on the pocket: a single golden gear.

"I promised you a new lab coat," Mother said.

I blinked back tears as I donned the lab coat. The rough yet familiar material wrapped around me. *A perfect fit.*

"Check the pocket," Father added knowingly with a wink.

I put my hand over the pocket, and felt what seemed to be a thin square. I reached in pulled it out.

White lines ran across the transparent surface, creating a grid. My fingers traced along the surface. A bright light appeared from the center displaying a holographic menu. "Welcome, Erin," it stated, the voice sounding like a woman's rather than a machine.

"This is the ArO-S, the newest technology from the Communications Division," Father said. "You are able to jot down notes while conducting experiments, capture images, or create projects. It has a database of information that you can access from any point on or off the planet's surface." He reached over and slid his finger down the machine and pressed two random points on it. It brought up a holographic directory of prelisted contacts, including Mother, Father and—*oh, Darwin*—Damon. "You can make calls to us anytime from anywhere."

"It is virtually indestructible," Mother added as Father dropped his ArO-S to the floor. A loud *clink!* echoed through the terminal. There was no way that such a frail object could survive such a fall. But as Father picked it up, I saw that it was completely unharmed.

"Basically, whatever you think it can do, it does that and more," Father continued with a laugh.

Gratitude swelled within me. I was leaving them, yet they were still there to help. A sudden confidence filled me. I was no longer frightened by the thought of leaving; now I wanted to do it. Darwin only knew how much this cost them, not just in material resources, but in letting me go. I threw my arms around them one last time, spattering tears all over their lab coats.

"Miss Erin!" Dr. Sharpe called out. I turned to look at him while still holding on to Mother and Father. "We are ready! Are you coming?"

I nodded. "Yes!" I replied. I turned back to my parents and withdrew my arms. Leaving their embrace was the hardest thing I had to do. I picked up my bag and ran to the airship as tears ran down my face. Dr. Sharpe stood in the open door of the airship, watching me.

He gestured into the interior of the ship. "After you, Miss Erin," he said.

I took a deep breath and stepped inside. The place felt as cold as the steel it was made of.

Or was that just me?

I turned back around to get one last look at my parents. I could see them waving as tears flowed down their faces like waterfalls, yet they smiled through the pain.

Their faces were the last I saw as the door to the terminal quickly shut.

CHAPTER EIGHT

"You seem quiet," he said.

I had spent the past several hours staring out the window. Dr. Sharpe's voice brought me back to reality. He sat straight on the red padded bench, staring at me with his probing brown eyes. I looked back out the window as we continued over the Atlantic Ocean, and the endless shades of blue that stretched for miles. I sighed. *Come on, Erin. You're going to be working with him every day now. Might as well get used to him.* I turned back to him.

"Sorry," I said awkwardly. "I'm not very sociable." I turned back to the window, mentally kicking myself. *Really? That's the best you can do?*

Dr. Sharpe raised his eyebrows. "Ah," he replied knowingly. "I see." He closed his eyes and took a deep breath. "I know this must be hard for you. But London is quite beautiful; I am sure you will like it. Have you ever been there?"

I turned towards him, raising an eyebrow. "You're actually making conversation with me?" I asked.

He shrugged. "I am going to be working with you," he said as traces of a smile lined his face. "I might as well try to make you feel comfortable, or even at home, if possible."

I avoided his gaze, heat rising to my cheeks. *I'm like a child being scolded.*

Dr. Sharpe laughed heartily, as if the rest of his body was laughing, too. "It is alright," he chuckled. "I know I can be intimidating. Everyone seems to be frightened of me for one reason or another."

"At least it gets the job done," I replied.

"More tea, Dr. Sharpe?" a robotic voice echoed. A thin, gray metallic automaton stepped from behind a purple curtain. It carried a silver tray with two white tea cups and an orb-like glass kettle filled with a dark liquid. Dr. Sharpe's gaze turned to the automaton. "Yes, please," he said as he waved it over.

The robot rolled forward. Its purple eyes seemed to glare at me as it set the tray on the table between Dr. Sharpe and myself.

"Now, now," Dr. Sharpe chided as if it were a disobedient pet. "Miss Erin is our guest. Be nice."

The automaton said nothing, but continued to stare at me as it retreated behind the curtain.

I laughed nervously. "What's with that robot?"

Dr. Sharpe rolled his eyes. "I recalibrated it from an old security system into my personal assistant. I believe he now uses those old security algorithms to protect me." He poured a cup of tea for himself. "Would you like a cup, Miss Erin?" he asked.

I shook my head. He shrugged and set the kettle back on its heater. He took a sip. "So tell me," he said seriously. *Oh, well. Back to business, I guess.* "What do you know about the Golgotha Project?"

I tried to look him straight in the eyes and match his intensity. I was pretty sure I failed. "I know that it was the first project undertaken by New Pangaea at the end of

World War Three. It's the main power source for the entire nation—"

"Stop there," Dr. Sharpe interrupted. "Those are the Gears themselves. I am referring to the project surrounding it in general. What is its purpose? Why have a whole project for the Gears in the first place?"

My eyebrows furrowed. "How do you expect me to know this?" I asked. "I haven't even started working with you."

Dr. Sharpe shook his head. "You are going to have to learn these things. You will not be working with me. I am merely the person in charge; there are several other Chemists and Mages who are involved."

"Wait," I interjected. "There are *Mages* working with you?" A mixture of relief and anxiety washed over me. *Maybe I can finally get some answers.* But did I really want to know what those answers were?

"Of course," Dr. Sharpe replied, eyeing me as he took another sip of tea. "Mages are no less worthy than any Chemist, despite what you might have learned. The fact that I, a Chemist, am in charge of the project is pure coincidence."

"No, no, sir. I wasn't implying anything like that at all. I..." I stopped. *No one, especially Dr. Sharpe, can know what happened.* "I've never met a Mage up close before."

Dr. Sharpe narrowed his eyes. *Damn it, he noticed my hesitation.* He closed his eyes as he took another drink. "Entirely understandable, Miss Erin," he replied, putting his cup down on the table. "No offense intended to you or your home city, but New Washington is especially... shall we say, prejudiced against Mages. A simple word driving a crowd of educated scientists to violence? It is disappointing."

I opened my mouth to defend my hometown, but immediately shut it. Whether I wanted to admit it or not, he was right. But was London any different? I looked out the window again. The night made the blue ocean appear almost black. Grey clouds rolled right alongside the airship. New Washington would often get very cold, especially at night. I missed its biting chill.

"Now," Dr. Sharpe continued, bringing my attention back to our conversation. He poured himself another cup of tea. "When we reach London, we will go straight to the Golgotha Laboratory. That is where we will begin your training. We still have about six hours left on our flight. I suggest you use it to get some sleep." He pointed to a door to my left. "Through that door are some beds; one has already been made for you." Dr. Sharpe took a sip of his tea and grimaced. "This tea is too cold," he said. He stood up and proceeded to walk towards the purple curtain. "E.M.E.T.!" he shouted. "Bring more tea!" He turned back to me. "I will wake you up once we reach London." His footsteps faded as he exited the cabin.

I took a deep breath and stood. My legs felt like gelatin from the hours I had been sitting; I almost tripped trying to catch my balance. I planted my feet firmly on the floor and walked to the door, but stepped back startled as the solid silver door automatically opened. It revealed a dark room with a series of approximately seven beds, all made the same way. The same white pillow and the same ugly red and yellow diamond blanket adorned each bed. *For the most prestigious program in New Pangaea, they really don't take care of their staff.* I chose the bed farthest from the door. I half expected the mattresses to feel like bricks, but when I sat down on it, the softness of the bed rolled over me. The reality of how tired I was set in. My eyes drooped, my yawns echoed through the room; I wouldn't be surprised if Dr. Sharpe could hear me from the other side of the airship. I really didn't care right now if the blankets were ugly as hell. London was waiting for me.

I was ready for London.

There I was, back in the same white space. Nothing had changed, but now when I looked at myself, I was wearing a solid white dress. The flowing skirt came down to my knees. A thick gold strap cinched my waist. The strap appeared to be woven from small white roses.

"Hello?" I called, scanning my surroundings for anything familiar. I ran across the vast space, my bare feet striking the floor without a sound. Was I walking on air?

This time, I did have a limited endurance. I placed my hands on my head and breathed. In through the nose, out through the mouth, *I coached myself. As I stood there, drenched with sweat, I noticed how cold the place was. Why anyone would wear a dress like the one I had on in such a cold atmosphere as this was beyond me. I wrapped my arms around myself, trying to keep warm.*

I felt a faint heat coming from my left. Everything almost seemed brighter on that side, too. Something inside me told me to follow it. The feeling was so strong it was impossible to ignore it. I turned and ran as fast as my legs could carry me. The heat grew warmer with each passing moment, until it was like a fire, and the room was as bright as the sun.

I saw it as my eyes adjusted to the brightness, and I saw that same gold anomaly I had seen just days before. Only this time, it was in some kind of containment tank. The rectangular tub was barely taller than me. The entity moved around frantically, searching for a way to escape. A million frantic voices rang in my ears.

My eyes fell on a small metal cart next to the tank. A number of assorted tools were lined up neatly in rows on it. There was also an ArO-S, some beakers and different multicolored chemicals. Off to the side was a rusty sledgehammer. My hands gripped the handle, but its weight pulled me downward.

The voices still echoed around me, speaking faster, faster. I heard different languages and accents, dialects that I had never even heard of.

"Don't worry," I said, determined. I finally got a firm grip on the sledgehammer. "I'll get you out of there."

I swung the sledgehammer as hard as I could, flinching as it loudly crashed into the glass. The voices' pitch changed as I slammed the sledgehammer into the walls of the tank twice, three times as the cracks grew. Finally, the glass fell to the floor in a million pieces and the gold anomaly escaped. Even though it had no face, I could feel its gratitude and happiness.

"You're welcome, I said, smiling. Everything vanished, and I was once again in the peaceful blackness of slumber.

I opened my eyes. The oranges of the sunrise dimly lit the bedroom. I sat up in bed and took a deep breath and stretched. *Another dream about the gold anomaly.* I ran my fingers through my hair and rubbed my eyes, exhausted but wide awake. I pulled the covers back in place to lazily make the bed. My tired mind still wandering, I made my way to the main cabin.

The room glowed with a blaze of early morning glory, cotton clouds rolling alongside the windows. I swore I could see a city underneath them.

A city...

I ran to the window, my mind suddenly alert. The clouds rolled away, revealing soaring skyscrapers, ornate bridges, crowded streets, and a great clock which towered above the city.

London.

CHAPTER NINE

"Come along, Miss Erin!" Dr. Sharpe shouted over the deafening noise of the airport. "We cannot be late!"

I jogged across the foyer dodging the countless people moving in various directions. I tried to keep up with him. People glared at me as I kept crashing into them. Yet Dr. Sharpe moved through the labyrinth of Londoners with ease. *This guy is crazy!*

"Late?" I asked, struggling to hear my own voice. "Late for what?"

"We are going to the Golgotha Laboratory," Dr. Sharpe replied as I finally caught up to him. "We are preparing you to start work as soon as possible. You can also meet the team."

I nodded as I gripped my backpack tighter. Thinking about working on the Golgotha Project was one thing. But the realization that I was here to actually work on it—that was a different story.

And I didn't want to take any chances after that dream last night.

I took a deep breath. "Okay," I said. "I'm ready." A crooked smile formed on Dr. Sharpe's face. "Well," he said, flicking imaginary dirt from his lab coat. "Let us be on our way. Shall we, Miss Erin?"

"Yes, sir." The doors opened.

"Welcome to London, Miss Erin," Dr. Sharpe said as he gestured with his hand to exit.

Tall buildings stretched into the clouded sky like metallic mountains. Sleek flying cars soared through the air, cleaner and smoother—and more common—than the ones in New Washington. I could make out the faint edge of one of the Gears towering in the sky. The streets below were narrow, but there were some people who preferred to walk in the shadows of London's skyline. A red double decker bus traveled along the road, occasionally stopping to pick up or drop off a passenger. I looked around, taking in the foreign sights and smells. And then it hit me.

Not everyone was the same.

The citizens of London would consider this to be a mundane fact of life, something that one wouldn't notice unless someone else pointed it out. Not everyone wore a lab coat, nor donned vine-like tattoos. It was a collective mix of both. *Perhaps London is different.* Then I noticed small differences. They walked on different sides of the streets. Any form of contact was avoided by Chemists and Mages alike.

Well, maybe not that different.

A glistening black car flew through the city, gently landing in front of us. My stunned reflection stared back at me, vanishing as the doors opened, revealing a luxurious interior, complete with shined leather seats and a rich burgundy carpet. A stout man in his late-thirties poked his head through the gap between the front seats and waved at us.

"'Ello!" the man called to us in a thick Cockney accent. His wide smile lit up his face. He waved his arms, signaling for us to climb in. "'Aven't seen you in a while!"

Dr. Sharpe nodded his head and smiled in return. "Hello, Mr. Brown," he replied.

The man continued waving his arms. "Get in, get in!" he shouted.

Dr. Sharpe turned to me. "Ladies first, Miss Erin?" he said as he gestured to the inside. I stepped into the car. Dr. Sharpe climbed in behind me as the doors shut. He took a seat facing me again.

"Fasten your seatbelts," Mr. Brown continued. "We're goin' up!" H slowly pulled back the lever next to him as the car began to pick up speed. The seatbelt failed to hold me in position. I could feel myself falling. Breathing heavily, I gripped the edges of the leather seats as we continued to pick up speed; eventually we caught up to the other flying cars. Out of the corner of my eye, I saw Dr. Sharpe once again staring at me, twisting his face as he tried not to laugh out loud.

"'Ey!" Mr. Brown's voice echoed from the front seat. "'O's the girl? 'As she never ridden in a flyin' car?"

Dr. Sharpe chuckled under his breath and cleared his throat. "Mr. Brown," he said, "this is Miss Erin Luciani, the newest addition to the Golgotha Project."

I nodded to Mr. Brown as I tried to slow my adrenaline rush. "Pleased to meet you."

"Ooh, not from London, ain't you?" He tipped his hat as he looked at me in the rear-view mirror. "Mister Orpheus Brown, at your service."

"Mister?" I asked. "So you're not a Chemist?"

A knowing smile lined Dr. Sharpe's face. "Miss Erin," he replied, "Orpheus is a Mage."

"Member of the Golgotha Project for twenty years!"

A mixture of awe and anxiety stirred within me. *A Mage! But what is he capable of? Can he know that I used magic?* I looked closer at his face. Sure enough, the signature vine-like tattoos ran up his neck, ending at his stern jaw. I gave Orpheus another small smile. "What do you do, Mr. Brown?"

"Please, call me Orpheus!" he said. His hazel eyes brightened his face, magnifying his smile. "And we'll cover that when we get to the Golgotha Lab!"

"While the Project itself is public information," Dr. Sharpe elaborated, "what we do is classified. The only one outside of the Golgotha Project who knows the inner workings of it is the Supreme Leader."

"I understand," I replied. "But why? I mean the only ones here are members of the Project."

Dr. Sharpe shook his head. "Technically, no," he replied. "You are only in training, Miss Erin. Official members of the Project either have earned the title of Doctor, or have trained as an apprentice. You were only a Chemist in training when you left New Washington. Therefore, that is what you are at this point. You will earn the title of Doctor at an accelerated pace. However, there is only so much we can divulge to you at this time."

I suppressed a groan. *What is with this guy? He doesn't make any sense. Why is he so... so...* I couldn't find the right word. "Yes, sir," I said bitingly. It was becoming more and more difficult to maintain my composure.

The remainder of the ride was filled with awkward silence. Not even Orpheus' garish Cockney accent helped to lighten the mood. I looked out the window to admire the scenery. Houses and skyscrapers and winding streets filled my view. A giant domed building with two twin spires dominated the smaller shops and homes surrounding it. Maybe it was the remnants of a church. Nearby, a winding river flowed underneath the ornate bridges which separated the two parts of London. My anxiety dissipated as I look upon the beauty of the city. *I can't believe I'll be living here.*

Out of the corner of my eye, I once again caught Dr. Sharpe's probing eyes staring at me. His piercing gaze examined me, as if I were some scientific experiment. I pretended not to notice, even though my skin began to crawl. *Should I even trust this man?*

"'Ey!" Orpheus shouted. "We're 'ere!"

The ride down didn't bother me as much, yet I still held on to the seats for dear life. Dr. Sharpe remained calm. *He's lucky he's so used to this.*

The car screeched to a halt. Orpheus turned to us, his hair a mess from the ride. "Well, 'ere we are!" he said with a smile. *Does this guy ever stop smiling?*

He pressed a button and the car doors opened. "I'll meet you inside after I park!" he bellowed. The noise from the streets of London assailed us. We climbed out of the car. Orpheus revved the engine and left in a rush of wind that blew my hair forward, temporarily obscuring my vision. I took in the full view of the Golgotha Laboratory as I gathered my hair behind my ears.

The golden bronze building stretched several stories high. Arched windows and doors wrapped around the structure with spires towering into the sky. The ancient Gothic architecture had withstood the test of time, war, and decay amid the modern city. Intricate sculptures lined the outer walls, completely preserved. The great clock I saw this morning stood at the far end of the building, as if guarding the secrets inside. The whole place seemed to welcome me as bells tolled in the distance.

"Beautiful, is it not?" Dr. Sharpe said, bringing me back. "They say that this was once a governmental facility—before New Pangaea, of course. Much of London was destroyed during the War... all of it, except for two places: an ancient castle and prison, an old church"—he pointed to a building similarly styled just across the street behind us—"and this. The Supreme

Leader vowed to always keep these places as part of New Pangaea's history by making this House the headquarters for the Golgotha Project." *I guess everyone's a little biased towards their home.* My heart still ached for New Washington.

Dr. Sharpe took a deep breath. "It would be unwise to keep the rest of the team waiting," he said. "Come." He walked briskly towards a massive arched door. Two guards, a Chemist and a Mage, stood at attention like silent stone statues at the door. Not even the bustle of the city could sway them. Dr. Sharpe nodded at them. The two guards stepped aside and opened the doors for us. A cool breeze welcomed us as we stepped inside. I was overwhelmed by the sight before me. The outside of the building was awe-inspiring and massive, and the inside was even more so with its ceiling reaching into the heavens.

"I take it you are enjoying yourself?" Dr. Sharpe asked, chuckling. I opened my mouth to respond, but no words came out. My senses were captivated by everything around me.

"Dr. Sharpe!" a woman's voice rang. "You're back!"

My attention shifted from the beautiful art to a young woman quickly approaching us down a flight of steps. It was obvious that she was a Chemist; the white of her lab coat stood against her chocolate brown skin. Her thick black hair was pulled up into a bun. A pair of wire frame glasses rested perfectly on her nose.

"Dr. Sharpe," she said, stopping in front of us," it's good to see you again. Everyone has been—" Her gaze fixated on me, her eyebrows furrowing. "Doctor," she said. "Who is this woman? She shouldn't be here."

I turned sharply to Dr. Sharpe. "Does anyone know about me?" I asked.

Dr. Sharpe narrowed his eyes at me. His intense gaze stopped my voice. He turned back to the woman. "Dr. Vermaak," he replied, "this is our new associate."

The Chemist raised her eyebrows. She turned to me and offered her hand. "Dr. Vynessa Vermaak," she introduced herself skeptically, "Mathematics Division and Member of the Golgotha Project." Her cynical attitude momentarily rendered me speechless. I choked out a weak "Pleased to meet you."

"She's so young, Dr. Sharpe, sir," she said. "Why choose her?"

Dr. Sharpe narrowed his eyes. "I believe that is my business, Doctor," he replied harshly. "The fact is that she is here now."

She shook her head. "Of course, sir," she said. "I understand, sir." She turned to me, attempting to mask her unease. "You heard him, Miss... um..."

"Luciani," I replied. "Erin Luciani."

Dr. Vermaak's eyes widened, showing off her dark brown, almost black, eyes. "Ah," she managed to stutter. "Yes... Erin..." Her surprise turned to thoughtfulness. "You look so much like your mother..."

"Dr. Vermaak!" Dr. Sharpe insisted. "May we go?"

She turned to Dr. Sharpe, her musing expression fading back into the business at hand. "Right away, sir. This way, please."

There were so many questions I wanted to ask. Why was no one aware of my coming? Why did everyone greet me with surprise or nervousness? And what did Dr. Vermaak mean by "You look so much like your mother?" I had no time to find answers for them at this point. But I knew one thing was for sure.

London was full of more questions than answers.

CHAPTER TEN

No words. I had no words.

Oh, Dr. Sharpe and Dr. Vermaak had plenty of words. Most of them were harsh whispers about me, echoing through the vast stone halls. I wasn't used to being the center of attention; it was always just my family and me. *Guess this comes with the territory.* I shrugged it off, deciding not to care. I could devote my time to studying the intricate details of the architecture.

The stone walls were stained grey. The columns stretched high until finally converging into arches high above me. Antique statues lined the halls. The ancient place was modernized with sleek, flat white lights along the sides of the arch while natural light entered through the colored windows dispersing the light as if through a prism. The two types of lighting created beautiful picture of life in New Pangaea, before and after the War. Many of the windows were clearly older than New Pangaea, regularly restored to their former glory by the steady hands of artisans. However, one recent window painted a picture of the Gears themselves. The mark of New Pangaca was ever present, even in a timeworn House like this.

"So," Dr. Vermaak said, breaking the silence, "where are you from?"

I kept my face blank. "New Washington," I replied, skeptical of her intentions. *The last time someone tried to be nice to me, shit happened.*

"New Washington," she repeated under her breath. "Interesting..." She shrugged. "What field did you specialize in?"

I turned away from her inquisitive gaze, my cheeks becoming warmer by the second. "I'm still in training," I replied softly. Realization flashed in Dr. Vermaak's eyes. She stopped cold, her eyes piercing Dr. Sharpe like daggers.

"You recruited a Chemist who's still in training!?" she shouted. "Why would you do that? What is the benefit in that?"

Dr. Sharpe scowled at her. Even though Dr. Vermaak was slightly taller than him, she still cowered in fear as if he were a giant. "I believe that is my call, Dr. Vermaak. She will receive her specialization in time. What matters is that she is here now and I expect you to treat her with the utmost respect." His eyes narrowed, seeming to morph into swords that pierced the poor Doctor. "And that means no more interrogations."

"I don't see the problem in getting to know her, sir," Dr. Vermaak replied.

"That is not the issue. The issue is when you embarrass her. Your questions—that, as well as the way you reacted to the fact that she had not specialized yet—implied she was not capable. Miss Erin has more potential than you realize."

Dr. Vermaak opened her mouth to speak, but closed it, thinking better than to cross Dr. Sharpe. He started walking again as Dr. Vermaak and I stood frozen in place. "Are you coming?" he asked, turning to us.

Dr. Vermaak flinched, still tense from his reprimand. She followed him, looked neither myself nor Dr. Sharpe in the eye. I followed closely behind her. Before turning around, Dr. Sharpe shot a brief glance at me. His eyes were softer this time, as if he was checking on me. The look in his eyes disappeared as suddenly as it had appeared. He continued down the hall, and the empty silence returned.

I stopped, confused. *Was that Dr. Sharpe's weird way of taking up for me?* I sighed, not wanting to dwell on it. Dr. Vermaak and Dr. Sharpe had walked a considerable distance. I picked up my pace to catch up with them.

We stopped in front of a great wooden door. Like the rest of the building, it stretched above me into an arch. Glass rectangles and triangles were scattered around it, stained to block the view from any prying eyes. Dr. Vermaak looked at me, her expression focused. "Everything beyond this door is confidential," she said. "Do you understand?" I nodded.

She smiled. "Welcome to the Golgotha Project," she said. She scanned the area, making sure that no one else was around, and then opened the door to another new world for me.

The room was not very wide even though the ceiling of the hall did reach high above me. There were some monitors along the walls, flashing holographic images above them, but there wasn't much else. One would think that the Golgotha Laboratory would have much more technology than this. *This is actually kind of... disappointing,* I thought to myself, not daring to say anything to upset the two Chemists.

"This isn't the actual main Lab, Erin," Dr. Vermaak said with a chuckle, noticing my disenchanted expression. "This is merely the Porch, where we check in every day." Dr. Vermaak and Dr. Sharpe walked towards one of the monitors. She placed her hand on the machine. The images scrambled until it revealed a complete profile of Dr. Vermaak: name, hometown, height, weight, hair and eye color, everything. Next to all of this was a picture of her sculpted face, bearing an almost cold expression, without even a smile. Green letters flashed over the profile. "Access granted," a woman's robotic voice said. Red lasers flashed ahead blocking an entrance. As the monitor's voice echoed through the chamber, the lasers disappeared. Dr. Vermaak waited at the entryway as Dr. Sharpe repeated the process.

"Simply place your hand here, and the system will recognize you as part of the Project," Dr. Sharpe said. He gestured to a dark green pad on the monitor. He chuckled. "Do not worry; I completed your profile on the way to London. The machine will not harm you."

A crooked smile lined my face at Dr. Sharpe's attempt at humor. I walked down the steps and gently placed my hand on the pad. The images scrambled, eventually morphing into static, before my profile appeared. Like Dr. Vermaak's and Dr. Sharpe's profiles, it contained the same information. But something about it seemed to throw me off. My profile picture wasn't just serious; it was lifeless, cold, as if it was a glimpse of a corpse. Below my picture in small font was an abbreviation: *P.O.I.* I tried to hide my shock as best as I could from Dr. Sharpe.

P.O.I? What the hell does that mean?

"Access granted," the emotionless voice repeated. "Welcome to Golgotha, Erin."

I flinched as Dr. Sharpe placed a rough, gloved hand on my shoulder. "The system does the same thing to everyone the first time they check in," he said. "It is nothing to be alarmed about." He gestured to the entrance. "You may go in." I followed them into the room, but stopped cold.

The hall seemed to stretch on forever. The arched, vaulted ceiling was higher than anywhere else in the building. Bright white lights hung from it. Beautiful windows similar to the ones I saw earlier lined the walls, letting in a vast array of colors of light.

Even in this age-old place, state of the art technology was abound, an anachronism to the awe-inspiring atmosphere. Projection tables sat on one side of the room, similar to the ones we had just passed, displaying everything from complex mathematical equations to historical timelines and even diagrams of different organisms. On the other side of the room, an assortment of natural items, elements, and metals rested on elegant rugs on the stone floor. Mages seated themselves around the objects, manipulating them as the items hovered in the air; one Mage even resurrected a dying plant. At the front of the room, a working model of the Gears sat underneath a giant stained glass window. My jaw dropped. Dr. Vermaak and Dr. Sharpe chuckled at my reaction.

We walked down the steps into the hall. The Mage who had resurrected the plant, a pale woman with fiery red hair, looked up as we entered. Noticing us, she immediately stopped what she was doing and ran towards Dr. Vermaak. Her green and violet robes flowed behind her, revealing the tattoos that cascaded down her long legs.

"Vynessa!" she cried, throwing her arms around Dr. Vermaak excitedly. "Did you see what I just did?" Her emerald green eyes radiated pride at her accomplishments. Upon seeing Dr. Sharpe, she distanced herself from Dr. Vermaak, clearing her throat. "I believe I have perfected a way to repair the Gears in the event of failed maintenance," she blurted nervously to him, attempting to repress her hyperactive nature. Her eyes fell to me. Her smile disappeared, replaced with confusion. "Who's this?"

"This is Erin Luciani," Dr. Vermaak replied, her smile betraying her professional exterior. "She is the newest addition to our little family."

I put up an interior wall, expecting a flood of comments about how "I shouldn't be here" and "She hasn't even specialized yet," or even "Not another Chemist." But unlike Dr. Vermaak, the Mage welcomed me right away. She shrugged and shook my hand enthusiastically.

"Hi!" she squealed, her voice thick with an unfamiliar but adorable brogue. "It's so exciting to meet you! I'm Chardonnay Neilly, but everyone calls me Charly. We're going to be best friends, I know it!"

"Calm down, Charly," Dr. Vermaak said, trying to hide her chuckle. "Erin still has a lot to take in. She's beginning her training here soon."

"Ooooh," she replied, the smile never leaving her face. "You're something special." Her contagious, happy-go-lucky attitude calmed me. But one thing kept biting at the back of my mind: *Why was a Mage being so kind to me? For that matter, why were both of the Mages I met so nice?*

"'Ey!" Orpheus called, his already loud voice echoing through the Lab. He jogged to us from the rug of elements. "You finally made it!" I was wonderin' why you were takin' so long!"

"We ran into Dr. Vermaak on the way here," I replied, finally able to get a word in. "And then we met Miss Neilly—"

"Please!" she interjected. "Call me Charly!" Dr. Sharpe glared at her angrily, and she lowered her head.

"Er... right," Orpheus continued. "Well, there's one more Mage you 'aven't met yet." He turned back towards the Mages' area. "Aya! Get over 'ere!"

A young woman sat on a rug in the corner of the room, moving her hands as gold energy manipulated a piece of metal. Tattoos flowed down her neck to her shoulders. She looked over at Orpheus as she heard her name. She let the metal drop and stood up, a small smile lining her face as she started to walk over to us. But when her eyes fell on me, the smile disappeared and was replaced with an ugly glare. Her dark brown eyes burned like fire. She stormed towards us, her dark hair flowing behind her. Her bronze skin shone in the lights of the room. But there was one thing I couldn't shake. Her face... I swore I had seen that face before. It was so familiar... why couldn't I place it?

"Aya," Orpheus said as she stopped. Everyone had gathered around me. "This is Miss Erin Luciani. She'll be joinin' us." Aya stood frozen, still glowering at me. Orpheus smiled awkwardly. "What's wrong?" he asked with a nervous, confused chuckle. "Aren't you goin' to say 'I?"

Aya scowled. "Hello," she said heatedly. "Welcome to Golgotha."

I frowned, putting up a defensive wall. *What's her problem?* I shook it off. As I looked at all of the Mages and Chemists around me, my defenses lowered and were slowly replaced with confusion. There were seven beds on the airship on the way here. I counted in my head everyone I had met. *Dr. Sharpe, Dr. Vermaak, Orpheus, Charly, Aya, me...*

"Isn't there a seventh person?" I asked Dr. Sharpe. Before he could open his mouth, footsteps echoed loudly behind me. *Finally, I'll have met everyone...*

"Hello, Dr. Sharpe!" an all too familiar voice called. *Oh, no! It can't be!* The blood left my face. My skin crawled. I wanted to vomit.

Please. Not him. Anyone but him.

I turned around. I thought I had left all of that behind me. I wanted to believe that, anyway. But there he was. That same blond hair and blue eyes. That same plastic grin. That same lab coat.

Damon.

CHAPTER ELEVEN

Son of a bitch.

"'Ello, Dr. Ritter!" Orpheus called. "What took you so long? 'ave you met Erin?"

I didn't move. I couldn't move. *How the hell? How was he here? And why?*

"Sorry for the delay, everyone," he replied. "I just got off my flight—" He turned to me, that strange yet familiar look in his eyes returning. "Why, hello, Erin," he said, his voice crawling on my skin like worms. "Fancy meeting you here."

The same fear and humiliation I felt on the day of the riot returned, threatening to overwhelm my senses. How did Damon get here, anyway? He had lived in New Washington ever since I was sixteen and in the middle of school…

Wait. All those years before. I knew nothing about his past. I sighed, exasperated. *I said I wanted answers. I guess the universe has a funny sense of irony.*

"What are you doing here?" I blurted out. "I thought you'd be in New Washington."

"What are you talkin' about?" Orpheus asked. "Dr. Ritter 'as been a member for years. 'e was assigned

overseas to learn about new security techniques…"
Realization lit his face. "'e went to New Washington!"

Aya clapped slowly, rolling her eyes. "Took you
long enough to put it together, genius," she replied
sarcastically.

Dr. Sharpe cleared his throat. The entire room fell
silent. "Dr. Ritter," he said, "it is good to finally have you
back with us. I trust your time in New Washington was
well spent?"

Dr. Ritter smiled charmingly. "Of course," he
replied. "I've learned so much. I even made a few
friends." He glanced at me and I couldn't stop from
shuddering.

"Glad to 'ave you back!" Orpheus boomed. "It
'asn't been the same without you."

"Well, I'm not here to make conversation,"
Damon said. His eyes focused on me. "I'm actually here
for Erin." I gulped, cringing at the thought of being alone
with Damon. *Oh, Darwin. Here we go.*

"The Supreme Leader wants to meet with her."

My jaw dropped. Once again, the Golgotha
Project had its way of making me speechless.

"W-what the—" Orpheus stuttered. "N-no one's
seen 'im in years! Why now?"

Damon shrugged. "I haven't a clue," he replied.
"All I know is that He wants to see her. Now."

Dr. Sharpe sighed. "I guess we will have to start
your training another time, Miss Erin," he replied. "We
are to comply whenever the Supreme Leader asks for
something." Worry flashed across everyone's faces. Well,
everyone except for Aya, whose scowl seemed to burn in
her eyes. *I'll just have to deal with her another time.*

Damon stood at the stairs, his hand stretched out.
"Come along," he said. "I'll take you." I quietly groaned
and shook my head. *Please, Darwin. Please don't let him
do anything.* I put on my best smile and walked up the

flight of stairs. The concerned and surprised faces of the rest of the team were the last things I saw as I left the room

For the first few minutes of walking, Damon was silent. The only sound in the entire hall was our breathing and the echo of our footsteps. I refused to look him in the eyes. His face was enough to bring back the memories of his harassment. I look around, trying to forget that he was walking next to me as we continued down the familiar hallway. The same statues, windows, and arches filled my vision. We were going back the way I came.

"So," Damon said, "are you going to ask what I'm doing here? Why I lied to you?" I kept walking in silence, fixating my eyes on the marble floor. He shrugged and continued. "It's just like they said: I'm in charge of security measures. When you first came in, you only saw those two guards, correct?" I rolled my eyes. *It's just like him to keep rambling even when it's clear that no one gives a shit.* "Ah, but it is only a ruse. The rest of the building is guarded by the most advanced weapons in the history of Chemistry and by Mages trained in the arts of reconnaissance and stealth. It was my idea," he added boastfully.

My anger boiled. I wanted nothing to do with this smug asshole, so why did he keep talking? I walked faster and faster, trying to keep ahead of him. Blood roared in my ears. I finally stopped and spoke my mind.

"I don't care!" I shouted. My voice echoed through the hall. "Why don't you just shut up!?" There was no response; just stillness. "Thank you," I whispered, relieved. There was still no answer. I frowned, becoming more aware of the deafening silence around me. I looked around. My eyes widened. I didn't recognize this place. *Where the hell am I?* No windows, no statues. And no Damon. The last fact should have delighted me, but I didn't want to be fully alone.

I'm lost.

Any rational person would stay put and wait for someone to come find her. But I had no time for that. The Supreme Leader—the most powerful person in New Pangaea—asked for me. I shrugged. I had no time to sit around and wait. I had to keep moving.

I took a deep breath to calm the anxiety within me. I thought back to when I first arrived, trying to remember how I got to the Lab itself. "Okay," I said aloud. "Let's just think about this." I drew a mental image of the path Dr. Sharpe, Dr. Vermaak and I had taken earlier, but stopped when I remembered what Father had said. *"Whatever you think it can do, it does all of that and more."*

Of course! My ArO-S! How could I forget?

I pulled out the thin transparent device from my pocket. I frowned. *How do I turn on this stupid thing?* I tried to recall how Father activated it. His fingers seemed to move randomly. I shook off my uncertainty. I couldn't afford to hesitate now. I slid my fingers down the surface of the ArO-S. *Please let this work.* Relief flooded me as the familiar menu opened up. "Welcome, Erin," a voice said. "What can I do for you?"

I scanned the menu. Contacts, programs, database... but where are the maps? "Where's the map of the Golgotha Lab?" I said. Just as I was about to give up, the images on the ArO-S began to blur. "Uploading map of Golgotha Laboratory," the machine said, as if it was replying to my request. A detailed map of the entire laboratory appeared. A white dot blinked on the translucent blue screen, indicating where I was. But something was odd about it. The blinking dot was outside the map, as if I wasn't even there.

Wherever I was, the map wasn't recognizing it.

I threw the ArO-S, frustrated. Not even one of the smartest machines in New Pangaea could help me. I looked around. The corridor was slim, lined with ancient paintings, as well as weathered old seats. The ceiling didn't reach high above me like the rest of the place. I took a deep breath as the feeling of claustrophobia started. I continued down the path ahead of me, but came to a sudden stop. I frowned.

The corridor ahead of me was a dead end.

Why would anyone build a place this way? What was the point of building a corridor with a dead end? I rolled my eyes. *I'll never understand ancient architecture.* I sighed and picked up my ArO-S, but something caught my eye as I turned around. The wall ahead of me looked identical to the rest of the walls in the House, but there was something... off about it. My stomach turned in knots. I squinted my eyes, trying to figure it out.

"We have been looking for you, Miss Luciani."

A deep, unfamiliar voice startled me. I nearly dropped my ArO-S again. I quickly spun around and took a sharp breath. A pale man in a black suit towered above me, his eyes hidden behind a pair of square shades. My eyes widened. I gulped. *A Silent One.*

"S-sorry," I stuttered, clumsily placing my ArO-S back in my lab coat pocket. "I-I got lost. Dam—Dr. Ritter was escorting me, but I seem to have lost him. I-I've never been here before."

The Silent One's face didn't change. He just stood there, staring at me like a predator ready to strike. Never had I felt so small. "Of course," he replied. "Right this way." He turned and walked away. I fought my unease and hastily caught up with him—or it. *He didn't even act human.*

We continued down the hall until we came to a magnificent octagonal lobby. Ornate patterns were scattered across the floor. Intricate sculptures, both large and small, lined the columns until they united on the golden ceiling. A great chandelier was suspended above me. On one side of the room, an enormous old painting hung on the wall. I recognized this place; I had come through here with Dr. Sharpe and Dr. Vermaak on the way to the main Lab. I shook my head, feeling stupid. *I can't believe I got lost after one wrong turn.* We kept walking down the same path through beautiful halls and rooms. *Mental note: make it a point to go exploring sometime.* Just when I thought we were leaving the Laboratory, we stopped outside a set of closed doors.

"You may go inside," the Silent One said. Neither his tone nor his expression had changed the whole time we had been walking. "I will call and let them know you have arrived." He opened the doors and held them as I stepped inside.

A fine carpet rested under my feet, lined with ornate patterns in blue and gold. The ceiling above me had a gold floral design. A border of swords and shields surrounded it. Behind me was an ancient fireplace that appeared to have been empty for years. A painting above the fireplace showed a man on a throne surrounded by angels. Gears surrounded the seat—a recent addition, judging from the slightly faded colors of the rest of the painting. A wooden model of the Gears rested on a sleek metal table, not unlike the ones in the main Lab. At the front of the room, an elegant throne rested on a platform. The sight of it made my legs tremble. I felt like I had walked more today than in all my years in New Washington. I looked around; no one was here yet. *Maybe I could sit on it... just for a few minutes...* I walked over to the throne and sat on it. The plush seat enveloped me. I wanted to fall asleep. I closed my eyes, allowing myself to slip into a light slumber…

"Ahem."

I shot up. Two Silent Ones stood next to a short thin woman. A glossy gray jacket and slacks matched her eyes. A black tie completed the ensemble. But it was her doll-like face that threw me off. Blonde curls cascaded down past her shoulders. Her pale face was free of any imperfections. Strange wires and anodes ran across her body, starting from her face and working their way down. Her lips curled into a smile as I stumbled to my feet.

"It is alright," she said, laughing. "I did not mean to startle you. Your journey must have been exhausting."

I stood up straight, attempting to appear professional. "I was told that the Supreme Leader wanted to see me," I said, swallowing. "Are you... it's just, I didn't expect you to be..."

She chuckled louder. "Oh, no, of course not," she replied. "That would be my Father. But He is ill at the moment, so He wished for me to come in His stead." She held out her hand. "I am LaVanna. It is an honor to meet you, Erin Luciani."

CHAPTER TWELVE

I furrowed my eyebrows, relieved… yet disappointed. It's not every day that you get to meet the daughter of the most powerful ruler in the world. But part of me wanted to meet the actual Man.

"I understand your concern, Erin," LaVanna said. "Do not worry; Father is fine and will recover soon. However, I believe I can be as much help to you as He can." She pressed one of the anodes on her temple. "Let us see now…" she said quietly, her eyes turning upwards to the right. "Ah," she said as she smiled, her white teeth shining in the light of the room. She faced me again. "Erin Luciani of New Washington. Twenty-one years old. Daughter of Thomas and Evelyn Luciani. Unspecialized Chemist in training."

My mouth hung open.

LaVanna chuckled. "Do not be alarmed," she said, gesturing to the machinery on her body. "This is merely the latest experimental model of the ArO-S. I am a walking computer, so to speak. Besides, I take my time to know every member of the Golgotha Project. You work not just for the people, but for my Father, and due to his deathly illness, I want to make sure that every detail of this Project runs smoothly." She walked around me, scanning me with her eyes. *Everyone seems to be eyeing me in some way*, I thought.

"Technically, we are not allowed to have unspecialized Chemists or untrained Mages on the Project," she said. "But Dr. Sharpe told me you are a very bright young woman. A little anxious, to be sure, but confidence is something that is built over time, so Father and I are willing to make an exception." She continued walking around. "He also said that you are especially skilled in physics, engineering, and astronomy. But you can only specialize in a maximum of two fields, and even just one field is exhausting enough. What to do..." She crossed her arms and stroked her chin. She stood there in silence until she snapped her fingers, her face brightening with revelation. "I have it! You shall specialize in Astrophysics! Therefore, I believe that the best course of action is to train you alongside Vynessa Vermaak and Makswell Sharpe. They are both quite skilled in engineering as well. I will ask them to add engineering training. You will be able to earn your specialization in as little as ten months. What do you say, Erin?"

I raised my eyebrows. "You're asking my opinion on this?" I asked. "But you're the daughter of the highest ranking Man in New Pangaea. I just follow yours and your Father's orders."

LaVanna smiled, shaking her head. "Specialization is a very important part of the life of a Chemist, Erin," she replied. "Had you stayed in New Washington, you would be receiving your specialization in due time. However, you are here, and you must be comfortable in your specialization. This decision will not only impact you, but the entire Golgotha Project, and thus all of New Pangaea."

I nodded. I thought back to my studies. I had learned about the topic before, but it was nothing more than a brief overview, and that was years ago. I swallowed, my body shaking. *I can't mess this up.* I took a deep yet unsteady breath...

LaVanna's face contorted slightly as she gripped her head, the lights beginning to flicker on and off.

I frowned, looking around the room as I tried to figure out why this was happening. LaVanna sighed exasperatedly. "Power outage," she murmured, clearly irritated. "Not again." She looked at me, her scowl quickly fading into a quirky smile. "I apologize, Miss Erin," she said. "This is quite embarrassing. I must go, anyway; Father may have an idea of how to solve this." She started to walk out the door.

I swallowed, gathering up my willpower. "Ma'am?" I called. LaVanna turned back to me, waiting.

"The Astrophysics specialization sounds wonderful," I said, adrenaline shooting through my veins. I could feel the temperature falling around me. *Shit...*

"Excellent!" LaVanna replied. "Talk to Dr. Sharpe when you return to the main Laboratory." She bowed her head gracefully. "It has been a pleasure speaking with you, Erin. I hope we meet again soon." She left the room perplexed.

I walked back up to the platform and collapsed on the throne, dizzy from the encounter and shivering from the icy chill of the room. I buried my head in my hands, hoping, praying that LaVanna didn't notice the slight temperature change. My eyes became hot, threatening to spill tears...

"Erin!" Damon's voice called. I sighed. I really didn't want him here right now.

He ran inside, breathing heavily as if he had been running. "I was looking all over for you! I was walking you here when suddenly you disappeared. What happened? And why is it so cold in here?" he added.

I shook my head and rubbed my eyes. I stood up, suddenly confused. He sounded genuinely concerned for me. I tilted my head. "Who are you and what have you done with the real Damon?" I asked.

Damon smiled. "Same as I've ever been," he replied, the concern in his voice disappearing. *Maybe I was just hearing things.* "So you didn't tell me: what did you and the Supreme Leader talk about?"

I got up and walked over to him, still keeping a safe distance despite the kindness he had displayed earlier. "Actually, it was His daughter that was here," I replied. "Apparently He's been very ill, so His daughter helps him manage things with the Project."

Damon's eyebrows furrowed. "That's odd," he said as we headed out the door. "I haven't heard anything about the Supreme Leader being sick." He shrugged. "It's just as well. It'd be pure chaos if the rest of New Pangaea knew that He was ill. Maybe that's why it was a Silent One who told me that He—or she, in this case—wanted to meet with you." He tried to reach for my hand as we walked, but I pulled it away from his grasp. Again I refused to look at him. "So what did *she* talk to you about?" he asked with a laugh.

"We talked about specializations. She said that it would be best if I specialized in Astrophysics. She also said something about additional engineering training, although it wouldn't be a specialization..."

Damon nodded. "Astrophysics and engineering, eh? Sounds like it could work. Dr. Sharpe oversees the Gears themselves, so he should know quite a bit about engineering. But we don't have anyone skilled in astrophysics. That'll be nice to have." My body tensed as I felt his hand on my shoulder. I wanted to push myself away, but the risk of getting lost kept me in place. *Then again, I could go back and explore that dead end...*

"Damon! Erin!" Charly's voice echoed through the halls. Her footsteps echoed as she rounded the corner and ran to us. Everyone's in the dining hall for dinner," she said, breathing heavily. "What took you so long?" A mischievous smile lined her face. "Is there something I should know about?" she asked playfully.

My eyes widened. I wanted to vomit. "Darwin, no!" I cried, moving as far away from Damon as I possibly could. Damon's quiet laughter at her comment made me want to punch him.

"Sorry," Charly said, hurt flashing across her eyes. "I was just asking. It's just that you two seem close."

"The only thing close about us is that we're from the same town," I replied, still reeling from her remark.

"Oh, Erin," Damon said, putting his slimy hand on my shoulder again, "come now. We were closer than that." I shrugged off his hand and rolled my eyes, attempting to restrain my anger and frustration. *You wish, asshole.*

"Well, like I said, everyone's in the dining hall waiting," Charly said, walking down the hall. "You can follow me if you want." She looked at me. "I'm sorry you've had to walk all day," she added with a smile. "It's tough at first. But you'll get used to it. If anything, Vynessa, Orpheus, Aya and I can help you. Well, maybe not Aya... Anyway, the dining hall is this way," she continued, pointing down the hall. Damon and I followed her down the massive corridor.

We walked in silence through hall after hall, gallery after gallery, eventually returning to the octagonal foyer I passed through earlier. Despite my nerves from the meeting and my frustration with Damon, the beauty of the lobby removed all of my negative energy. *Perhaps I did make the right decision coming here.*

"The dining hall is straight ahead," Charly said, leading us down another long hallway. It seemed to look the same as the corridor with the dead end: old and new paintings, seats lining the walls. A pair of doors were opened at the end of the hallway, revealing a large room.

The creamy white floor was a stark contrast to the dark, squared ceiling above me. Black triangles ran around the edges of the floor, separating it only slightly from the walls. Ornate patterns were sculpted into the arches above each doorway. Statues of the influential men and women who gave birth to the Golgotha Project lined the walls, each either holding or standing in front of, or holding a model of the Gears. At the center of it all sat a grand metal table covered with antique dishes and colorful food I had never seen before. Smoke rose out of the food, as if the table itself was cooking it and keeping it warm. Mages sat on one side, Chemists sat on the other. Dr. Sharpe sat at the end of the table, smiling as we entered.

"Hello, Miss Erin, Dr. Ritter, Miss Chardonnay," he said, greeting us as he gestured to the three empty chairs around the table. "Please, join us."

Charly walked to one side of the table and sat between Orpheus and Aya. Two empty chairs sat next to Dr. Vermaak. A licentious smile crossed Damon's face as he eyed them. Dr. Vermaak stood up before Damon could even sit down.

"Dr. Ritter," she said with a smile, her hands on her chair. "Why don't you sit next to Dr. Sharpe tonight? It's been a long time since you've been here, and you've had poor Erin all to yourself for the past five years." Damon opened his mouth in protest. "Please, I insist," she added, cutting him off. He sighed and rolled his eyes as he took her seat. Dr. Vermaak sat down in the middle chair between Damon and me. Her sympathetic eyes locked onto mine. *Thank you,* I mouthed to her.

"Now," Dr. Sharpe said, reaching for the food. "Let us eat."

Everyone went for the food as if they hadn't eaten in days, reaching for everything from pies to meat, even different soups. Recipes from all over New Pangaea rested on the table; I smiled as I caught a glimpse of the same sort of cake Mother would always make for me for my birthday. The same butter cream frosting and flowers adorned it. I sighed, comforted by the familiarity, but sobered as I realized that I had never actually eaten any of the cake she made for me for my twenty-first birthday. It sat on the table, beckoning for me to bask in its rich sweetness, but it was too far away.

"Please pass the cake," Dr. Vermaak said, noticing my feeble attempts at reaching it. The top of the table rotated like a carousel until the cake arrived right in front of my plate, receiving complaints from a gorging Orpheus. I happily cut a slice of it.

"It's a little hard to get used to," she added, gathering a spoonful of meat and vegetable soup for herself. "We eat here three times a day, but we always have some fruit and light refreshments available in case you need something in the middle of the day." She pointed jokingly at Orpheus. "Although you might have to beat Orpheus to them before he eats it all."

"'Ey!" he replied, laughing as he waved a piece of meat in the air. "At least I don't have to deal with your sorry stick-up-your-arse attitude! Can't imagine 'ow I'd fare with you as a Mage!" The entire table roared with laughter as Dr. Vermaak rolled her eyes, but even the serious Chemist couldn't help chuckling along with them.

"Calm down, everyone," Dr. Sharpe shouted. Everyone fell silent as his voice echoed through the room. All eyes were on him; it was just the same as when he arrived in New Washington. "Erin," he said, staring at me, "how did your meeting with the Supreme Leader go?"

I opened my mouth to speak, but shut it. I didn't know what to say. *Should I tell them that I met with his daughter instead? Do they know about His illness?* I cleared my throat. "The meeting went well," I replied, not specifying with whom. "We discussed my specialization. Sh—it was recommended that I specialize in Astrophysics, while receiving additional training in engineering. Apparently, I can receive my specialization in as little as ten months."

Dr. Sharpe raised his eyebrows. "Ten months," he mused. "That is quite a tall order, sooner than even I expected. He must really want you to be specialized as soon as possible." He took a bite of some breaded beef. "Did He say with whom you would train?"

"I am to train with you, actually," I replied. "You and Dr. Vermaak."

Dr. Sharpe froze, his fork halfway between the plate and his mouth. He put it down and took a deep breath. "I have not trained a Chemist in a long time," he said, clearly surprised. "So you will forgive me if I am a little out of practice." He turned to Dr. Vermaak. "Do you feel you are qualified to train her?"

She nodded. "I am a servant of the Supreme Leader," she replied without hesitation. "If He wishes me to train our new recruit, then that is what I will do."

Dr. Sharpe gave a small smile as he shifted his attention back to me. "Then it is settled," he said, curiosity flashing for a moment across his face. "We will start your training in the morning."

CHAPTER THIRTEEN

I sat in silence for the remainder of dinner. The voices of the other Mages and Chemists overwhelmed me, muddied together like a wall of sound. I was invisible to this crowd. No one paid attention to me, which I surprisingly appreciated. Ever since Dr. Sharpe and the Golgotha Project came into my life, everyone eyed me, wanted to speak with me. Aya was the only one staring at me, her eyes cold and angry. *What the hell is her problem?* I thought, trying to ignore her piercing gaze.

"I'm tired," Charly said as she yawned and stretched her arms. "I'm going to sleep. Who's with me?"

Dr. Vermaak raised her hand with a weary smile. "I'll follow you," she replied as she stood up and headed for the doors. Orpheus and Damon followed closely behind.

Charly stood up and started walking with Dr. Vermaak, but stopped and turned back to me. "Are you coming, Erin?" she asked. "I can show you where to go, if you want."

"Sure," I replied. "Thanks."

"I don't mind at all," she replied. "Like I said, I'm here to help." I stood up and followed her out to the hall.

"Oh, how I wish you were a Mage!" she cried as she practically skipped down the hall. I almost had to jog to keep up with her. "Oh, well! I'm sure you'll do great with your specialization!"

She continued rambling. Her exuberant spirit was a comfort, though also mildly unsettling. When I finally caught up to her, I put a hand on her shoulder. She turned back to me, her eyes lit with energy that rivaled anything I had ever seen. I didn't want to hurt her, but I had to know.

"Why are you so nice to me?" I asked. I gestured to my lab coat and her robes. "I'm a Chemist, you're a Mage. Our people don't get along. So why do you treat me as one of your own?"

Pain radiated in Charly's eyes as she dropped her eyes to the floor. Her shoulders slumped. Her bright red locks fell across her face as she turned away. After a few brutal moments, she gathered her hair back behind her ears. Her bright and joyful expression returned as if I had never asked that question. "That may be how things are out there," she said, taking my hand. "But here, we're all we have. I won't lie, it does get lonely in here, working, sleeping, eating, with little time for ourselves. That kind of life… you can't live like that alone." She dropped her hand. "Besides," she added, "you're different. Much different than the other Chemists out there." She skipped off down the hall as I trailed closely behind her.

Charly's words warmed my heart, but that last statement drove through my chest like an ice pick. Did she know about my magic? Does anyone know? I shook my head. *Come on, Erin. You're being ridiculous.* I sighed. *Why do I always have to freak out over everything?*

The rest of the way to the bedroom I didn't say a word, simply watching the sunset through the elegant windows as Charly chattered about Darwin only knows what. The rich, deep colors bled through them, giving the hall a gorgeous golden glow. My skin reflected the light's warm hues. The breathtaking skyline of London darkened in contrast to the sun's final farewells to the Earth, streetlights and skyscrapers beckoning the coming of the Moon. As the sky darkened, the outline of the Gears became clearer and clearer, until their full silver glory reigned amongst the stars.

Charly's hand softly grasped mine. "Erin," she said with a laugh. "Aren't you going to bed?"

Her voice brought me out of my trance. "Yeah," I said, nodding. "Yeah, I'll be there in a minute. Just lost myself for a second."

"I understand," Charly replied, nodding back. "London is beautiful. Makes me miss my old home sometimes." She yawned. "I don't know about you, but I'm exhausted. It's definitely been a long day." *Don't I know it,* I thought. "Come on," she said, leading me through another pair of doors.

The great room was like a cavern. Elegant and detailed patterns of many colors spread out along the floor, matching the ornate ceiling above. Aged artwork lined the walls, from great battles to beautiful men and women dressed in luxurious, dignified regalia. Each painting was modified to include a model of the Gears. Beautiful windows rested above the artwork; the muted colors of twilight bled through them.

Beds were on both sides of the room, four on my left and three on my right. Matching nightstands and dressers sat on either side of each bed. But I groaned inwardly as I noticed that every bed was exposed. *Damon's going to see me naked,* I thought. *Fantastic.*

Charly sped past me, running to the bed closest to me. She waved her hands above her nightstand, and a slideshow of pictures appeared. Luscious reds, blues and violets swirled behind them. I could faintly see the outline of what appeared to be a force field as I looked closer at the beds. Charly stretched out her arm above her, and dragged her hand across the force field to create a solid, dark red wall. Dr. Vermaak and Aya were already at their beds, leaving one at the far end of the room for me.

My "bedroom" was half the size of my room back home. I sighed, mentally correcting myself. *This is my home now.* The blankets had the same ugly pattern as the ones on the flight here. The bed itself was much larger— and much more comfortable, I thought to myself as I sat on it. I laid my head on the pillow, rubbing my face against the silky pillowcase. The mattress seemed to conform to my every movement.

As I moved, it became harder to stretch out my arms. I looked down and realized I was still in the same outfit from when I arrived. A coat hook rested on the wall next to my bed. Sighing, I reluctantly climbed out of bed. I took out my ArO-S and placed in on the dark maple nightstand before hanging up my lab coat.

I started unbuttoning my blouse when I remembered that I had nothing to wear to bed. I searched around the room, hoping that Mother was right about them providing me with new clothes. I checked the dresser on the opposite side of the bed. I opened the top drawer and sighed with relief as I saw several pairs of pastel silk pajamas. I pulled out the top ensemble—a pale pink long sleeve and pants set—and threw it on my bed. Exhaustion overwhelmed me as I undid the last of my buttons and my bra and dropped them both next to the bed.

"How was your first day, Miss—?"

Instinctively, I turned around, but stopped cold at the sight.

Dr. Sharpe stood in front of my room, his eyes wide and his face as red as the force field wall.

The wall. I never closed the wall. *Shit.*

Blood rushed to my face as I froze, my breasts in full view of Dr. Sharpe. He averted his eyes, his blush deepening. Looking around the room, the hall started to become hot as I realized that I had exposed myself to every person on the Project. Dr. Vermaak sat in her bed, her jaw wide open in shock. Aya laughed. Damon stared hungrily at me.

The temperature steadily continued to climb. "Um...uh..." My choppy speech only managed to make Aya laugh even harder, and earn irritating "Awws" from both Dr. Vermaak and Orpheus. When I finally managed to gather my bearings, I covered my naked chest. "Um, have a good night!" I quickly blurted. I desperately tried to copy Charly's movements until I finally managed to close the wall.

I finished putting on my pajamas in silence. Not even the softness of the silk could soothe me. I let my head fall into my hands, fighting back the tears that were starting to boil in my eyes. I pulled back the covers and laid in bed, wanting to just fall asleep and forget this whole thing never happened.

"She's so pathetic," I overheard Aya say. "Pathetic and sheltered. What Dr. Sharpe sees in her is completely beyond me."

I forgot about my earlier resolve as I let my tears fall onto my pillow. How I wanted to give up, to go back home to my family. They may have been the only people I knew other than Damon, but at least I knew that they would never treat me with such hostility. I may have not been able to have such freedom, but the idea of security seemed awfully tempting, especially now. I wiped my tears and closed my eyes. My silent sobs were the last thing I heard before I drifted off to sleep.

I was back in that white field. I sighed. Not again, *I thought, dreading whatever was to come of these dreams in the world of the living this time. Once again, I wore that same white dress, and my bare feet stood on the white nothingness. I looked around, but saw no sign of the* gold mist or of anything that would lead me to it. I turned and flinched in surprise as it suddenly appeared before me. It moved quickly and swirled around me, as if thanking me once again for the previous dream. I tilted my head. "What do you want?" I asked. The mist stopped, the gold still churning within it, before speeding off and leaving me behind.

"W-wait!" I called, running after it. "What's going on?" A bright flash blinded me. I dropped to my knees, shielding my eyes from the light. But when I opened them back up, I was no longer in that empty whiteness.

I was in the same corridor I had been in earlier.

I got back up, wincing as the hard floor chilled my feet. I looked around; the same old paintings, the same tattered seats filled my view. Ahead of me was the dead end. The gold mist hovered next to me. It slowly moved forward until it did something particularly odd.
It moved straight through the wall.

My eyes widened. I was about to dismiss it as a dream. But I remembered the quality of these dreams, and the real life consequences each one delivered. I narrowed my eyes, deciding to apply what I had learned as a Chemist and perform an experiment.

I examined the wall next to me, taking into detail the color, the cracks in the bricks, the texture. I placed my hand on an empty space of the wall next to me. The brick wall felt firm against my palm. I knocked on it to make doubly sure that it was indeed solid; it stood up against the test. Turning my attention to the dead end, I slowly walked forward and examined it. It seemed to match the wall in every way. I placed my hand on it, checking the texture and pressing my hand against it. Nothing happened. I knocked on it, and it still was solid. I sighed. Perhaps it's nothing, I thought, disappointed. But just as I was about to walk away, the gold mist came back through

*the wall. "Is there something else I haven't considered?"
I asked it. I rubbed my eyes and scoffed at myself. I'm
talking to a gas, I thought.*

*The mist hastily surrounded my right hand,
compressing itself around it until my hand glowed with its
warm energy. Anxiety started to overwhelm me, causing
the fog to unwind, until a small voice rang in my ears.*

Be not afraid.

*It was the first time I recalled the young Mage's
last words since the riot outside the Lab in New
Washington the day I first met Dr. Sharpe. I considered
her words. Was she telling me not to be afraid of magic?
And if she was, how did she know I was capable of it? I
took a deep, resolved breath. I knew there was something
behind this wall. I had tried everything that my life as a
Chemist had taught me. There was only one way now.
Once again, I placed my hand on the wall. But when I did,
my eyes widened.*

My hand had slipped through the wall with ease.

*I knew it! There was something suspicious about a
random dead end! My hypothesis had proven correct! I
partially withdrew my hand and stared at the gold energy
around it. The mist burned brighter than I had ever seen it
before. Curious, I used all of my willpower and asked it to
spread around my entire body.* I need to get behind this
wall, *I thought. I gasped as the sentient energy appeared
to listen to me, slowly flowing down my arm, around my
shoulders, down my other arm and my legs, until it
covered my torso and eventually my head. My fears
vanished as the magic shielded me from the ordinary laws
of nature. I slowly stepped through the wall, eager to see
what was beyond this solid door—*

I shot up out of bed. A loud series of knocks had
awoken me from my slumber. I rubbed my eyes and
climbed out of bed. I rubbed my finger on the ArO-S. The

main menu opened and displayed the time in the right hand corner. *3:30 a.m.*

I shook my head as the knocks grew faster. *Who the hell would wake someone so early?* I shrugged, figuring that this was something part of the life of the Golgotha Project. Maybe they woke obscenely early to begin their work? I walked to the force field wall and opened it.

Aya stood there, her eyes burning.

"It's 3:30 in the morning," I said, yawning. "What's going on?"

Aya said nothing, but continued to stare at me. Suddenly, I flinched as she quickly seized my wrist with an iron grip and dragged me down the hall towards the doors.

"What the—!?" I said quietly, not wanting to wake anyone. "I know you hate me for some odd reason, but—"

"Shut the hell up," Aya snarled as she yanked me out the doors. She turned, grabbed my shoulders and pinned me against the wall.

"Ouch!" I cried. "What's—?"

"I said shut the hell up!" Aya spat, covering my mouth with her hand. "Now listen, Erin, and listen well. I know who you are. I know what you've done."

I gulped. *Oh, shit.*

"You can't even begin to understand how much I hate you," she continued.

"Why—?"

Aya clenched her fist and punched me, pain shooting from my jaw. The metallic taste of blood filled my mouth. "Shut the fuck up," she growled. "I'm only going to say this once: if you ever cause suffering and destruction here, I will personally gut you and slit your throat. I have no clue why Dr. Sharpe thinks you're so special, but there's nothing I can do about it now. So let's do each other a favor and leave each other alone. If you don't start shit, then I won't. It's as simple as that." I winced as her grip tightened. "Is that clear?"

I nodded, not wanting to invoke her wrath again.

She let me go. "Good," she replied, her calm voice a stark contrast to her threatening tone just moments ago. "Now go back to sleep. We wake up at exactly 7:00 a.m., and Dr. Sharpe doesn't like it when people are late." She walked back into the room. I followed behind her.

I walked slowly back to my bed, still in shock over her warning. I wiped my mouth, and sighed as a red stain tinged my sleeve. When I reached my bed, I made sure to make the force field wall—I definitely didn't want another episode like a few hours ago—and climbed back into bed. I had no dreams or disturbances for the rest of the night.

CHAPTER FOURTEEN

"Again," Dr. Sharpe said. "What is the Cosmic Microwave Background?"

It had been two weeks since my first day at the Golgotha Project. The time had passed by uneventfully: Aya was still a royal bitch, Charly was still happy, Damon was still a pervert. Even Dr. Sharpe remained the same enigmatic leader. But the dream I had that first night still resonated in my mind. The dead end... whatever was beyond it... I wanted to explore it. But the training kept me so busy that by the time I finally had some time to myself at the end of the day I used it to sleep. I often thought about that dream. I would frequently lose focus during my training to ponder what was beyond the wall, and why someone would seal it off...

"Erin!" Dr. Vermaak shouted.

I turned back to them, startled by her loud voice.

Dr. Sharpe shook his head and stared at me. "You need to focus! The Supreme Leader wants you to be ready in ten months! And He does not like to be kept waiting."

"I'm sorry," I squeaked out.

Dr. Sharpe sighed, exasperated. "Do not apologize," he replied. "Just do it." He brought my attention back to the projection in front of us. "Let us start from the beginning... again," he said, dragging his hand across the projection until a portrait of the Earth and the Gears rotating around it materialized. "What do you see?"

"The Earth and the Gears," I replied.

"Good," Dr. Sharpe said. "What else do you see? What keeps the Gears where they are?"

I froze, desperately trying to recall what I learned. *Come on, you went over this just last week!* I tried to remember something, anything about physics... I'm supposed to be good at this, for Darwin's sake! I felt the weight of anxiety on my shoulders, forcing me down... *Down.*

"Gravity!" I cried in revelation. "Gravity and inertia! The Gears travel at just the right speed to orbit the Earth, like the satellites we used to build a thousand years ago! Those two forces, gravity and inertia, are what keep the Gears in place!"

Dr. Vermaak gave a small smile and applauded. "Very good, Erin," she said. I smiled. "But what kind of orbit do the Gears have?"

My smile immediately disappeared. *Shit.* "Um..."

The lights began to flicker. *Again?*

Everyone stopped what they were doing and stared as not only the lights, but the Chemists' technology flashed over and over until everything in the room shut off.

"What the 'ell is going on?" Orpheus asked as he formed a ball of light in his hand.

"Just another power outage," Dr. Vermaak replied, sighing as she scoured the room for a solution.

My eyebrows furrowed. I turned to Dr. Sharpe. "Power outage? I thought the Gears produced unlimited energy."

"So did we," Dr. Vermaak replied.

"But for the past several hundred years, we've had numerous blackouts, some of which lasting upwards of three months," Damon added, walking towards me. "The longest one we ever had was for six months. A lot of good people wound up dead."

"A world without power is a dead world," Orpheus said.

"One hypothesis that we've been testing is that the Gears have been slowing down during that period of time," Damon continued. He wrapped his arms around me. I wanted to throw up. "Don't worry though; I'll protect you from the darkness." I pushed him away, glaring at him.

Dr. Sharpe cleared his throat. "That has been the Project's main focus for the past several hundred years. We believe that your skill in physics—and your eventual specialization in Astrophysics—may help shed some light on this situation."

I gulped. *No pressure.*

"Now," Dr. Sharpe said. "We must get the power turned back on. Miss Erin, can you walk with Orpheus and find the central power hub?"

I nodded. "Yes sir," I replied, still reeling from the amount of pressure I felt.

Orpheus stepped up next to me. "Just follow me, miss," he said. "You won't get lost, I promise." I smiled at Orpheus' comforting words. I followed him as we walked out of the Lab.

"Where is the 'central power hub,' anyway?" I asked Orpheus. His stride was quick but graceful, and I struggled to keep up behind him.

"We're goin' to the clock, ma'am," he replied with a smile, slowing down so I could keep pace with him. I smiled, too; I had grown used to the kindness that was displayed to me by the Mages. Well, most of them, anyway.

"This room is beautiful," I said, admiring the designs and colors of the octagonal foyer as we passed through it.

"That it is, ma'am," he replied. "We 'ad nothin' like this back in my home."

We took a left turn and walked down the same corridor into the dining hall. The table was filled with an assortment of vegetables and fruits, as well as different drinks. "No, it's not 'ere," Orpheus quipped. "We've still got a ways to go." He grabbed an apple as we crossed the room and wiped it on his robes. The juices dripped from his mouth has he bit into the fruit. I chuckled. *I guess Dr. Vermaak was right.*

We paused at a brick wall below one of the opulent arches. He stopped me with his hand. "Give me a moment, miss," he said as he placed his hand on it. His eyes focused on the wall.

And then everything was washed over with grey.

Orpheus' hands glowed with a silver energy, growing brighter every second. But the rest of his body radiated chocolate brown. The silver flowed down his arms like a river, slowly replacing the brown; the more forceful he became, the faster the colors flowed, until his entire body was covered with silver. A white light burst from his hands, causing the bricks to part, forming a pathway.

Just like that, the colors faded away.

"We still 'ave a ways to go," he said, turning to me. He frowned, his concerned expression accenting his wrinkles. "Are you alright, miss?" he added. "You look ill. You can sit down 'ere, if you want. I can 'andle it myself."

I shook my head quickly. "No, no, I'm fine," I replied as I cleared my throat. "I just didn't know there was anything beyond that. And I've never... you know..."

"Ah," he said, nodding his head in understanding. "You've never seen magic up close before." He smiled. "Magic is a living, breathing energy. It just so 'appens to flow through us Mages." *Like light through a prism,* I thought. "But like anything in this world, it can be

102

misused." He gestured towards the dark passageway. "After you, miss?"

The temperature dropped considerably as I stepped inside and walked down the short corridor. Darkness enveloped me; the old stone around me made the place seem more like a cavern than the Headquarters I had begun to call my home. The room smelled musty. I could feel dust particles flowing into my nose as I breathed and sneezed.

"Need some light, miss?" Orpheus asked as he held out his hand. A ball of light began to form above his palm. Unlike the splitting of the wall, his eyes were gentle and calm, almost as if he were beckoning a small child. The ball of light grew larger until it floated away from his hand and above our heads like a miniature sun.

The room was indeed like a lost cave. The ceilings and walls stretched far and wide. Platforms lined the sides of it. Old indentations in them marked places where furniture once sat. The floor felt sticky under my feet, faded in spots where a carpet once had been.

"Where exactly are we going, Orpheus?" I asked as I followed Orpheus to the back of the room.

"Why, to the clock tower," he replied as he stopped in front of an old door. It creaked, sounding as if it could break any moment as he opened it. "Only way to get there without attractin' attention is through this old part. We 'ave to take a few more turns and climb a few stairs, but we'll get back before dinner, I promise." The door shut behind us as we walked through it.

The ball of light remained over our heads, and I was glad it did; the light banished some of the thick darkness that enveloped the hall. For some strange reason, everything was boarded up, worn down from countless years of negligence. The walls were nothing more than crumbled ruins. Only individual splotches of colors remained on tired paintings. The windows were covered with stone. But why would they want to forget this part of the Headquarters? Was this what waited for me behind that wall?

We kept walking until we reached another door. But unlike the rest of the abandoned halls we had traversed through, it was the only thing that seemed to stand the test of time. It didn't even groan as Orpheus walked through and opened the door for me. The ball of light illuminated the tower, revealing a winding set of stairs. *Great. More walking.*

"Come on," Orpheus said cheerfully as he waited at the first step. "No time to waste." I rubbed my legs, dreading the ache I'd feel tomorrow.

Orpheus kept up his cheerful attitude as we climbed the steps, his boisterous voice echoing through the cramped space. At first, walking up the staircase wasn't too bad. But my complacence soon faded away; as we went higher, the air became thinner as I struggled to breathe. I could see Orpheus' concerned stare out of the corner of my eye.

After what felt like an eternity of climbing, we finally stopped at the front of a slightly rusted metal door. Orpheus turned to me, his eyes brimming with excitement.

"This isn't where the power 'ub is," he said. I inwardly groaned, my legs burning from the trek up here. "But I wanted to show you this. Consider it your initiation into the Golgotha Project." He laughed as he gestured to the door. "Go on." I opened the entryway, but raised an eyebrow. It was nothing but a bright white corridor.

Orpheus pushed me further. "You 'ave to go around the corner," he said enthusiastically. I sighed and did as he said. My jaw dropped as I rounded the corner.

The face of the great clock.

The entire room was covered in white. Sunlight poured in through the tinted white glass, accenting the black numbers and the many circles within circles. The city below seemed microscopic as I gazed out of the clock's face. Several bright lights were attached on the wall behind the face, probably to illuminate the clock at night. The sheer brightness of the place reminded me of the white space in my dream. I was on top of the world, reaching with all my might to the heavens.

"Enjoyin' yourself?" Orpheus asked, suddenly appearing next to me. I nodded, the smile not once leaving my face.

Orpheus chuckled. "I knew you'd like it. Everyone on the Project 'as been up 'ere at least once. Figured it was your turn. Besides, you look like you could use a break," he added, seemingly concerned.

Tears welled up in my eyes. "Thank you," I choked, wiping them away.

"You're very welcome, Miss Erin," he replied. "Now, we need to fix the power 'ub. We don't 'ave that much further to go." I walked with him out the door and up the steps, still basking in that adrenaline rush.

It wasn't long until Orpheus stopped at another door. "This is it," he said. He turned to me. "Aren't you glad we're finally here?"

I laughed, nodding slightly. "Just a little bit."

He opened the door. "Come on in," he said. "We've got work to do."

The place wasn't as white as the room of the clock faces, but light still beamed in from a few smaller windows. It was larger, though, and it felt good to be able to finally breathe. The room was absolutely full of gears. But what struck me the most was that the room was completely silent, save for our breathing. Shouldn't the gears be spinning? Shouldn't there be the ticking of the clock?

"Can you come over 'ere?" Orpheus asked, stopping in front of a block of gears. "This is where I'm goin' to need you."

"Sure," I replied as I walked over. "What do I need to do?"

He pointed to a conspicuous piece of metal on the block. "We need to get these lovelies spinnin' again. This is where I'll need your 'elp." He looked at me. "Maybe this'll 'elp in your trainin', too," he added.

"I don't do magic," I said, my eyes unconsciously moving away from his otherwise kind gaze. "I'm not a Mage."

"You were really sheltered, weren't you?" he asked. "Listen, the only way we can solve this is by workin' together. Now, what does your freaky science thing say about moving things?"

"Motion?" I thought back to what I learned in school. I easily pulled one of the first laws I learned out of my memory. *An object standing still will stay that way until it's acted upon by an outside, unbalanced force.* I turned my attention back to Orpheus, feeling more confident than I had been over the past couple of weeks. "If we want these gears moving again, we need to make them move," I said with conviction. "But how do we get them moving? Push them?"

He shook his head. "These babies are really old," he replied. "I don't want to break them."

"Well, we need some old fashioned kinetic energy," I replied. I walked over to the gears. "Let me examine them." I placed my hands on the gears, analyzing their makeup, their texture, anything that could help me. Noticing the rust on them, I knew that Orpheus was right about not being able to push them. They needed a stimulus to start moving again. But with the power being out, there were no stimuli. There couldn't be one without the other. I had no idea what to do.

"Damn it, why won't you start!" I shouted, gripping the gear as hard as I could.

A bright light blinded me. The explosion of energy sent me flying backwards, crashing into Orpheus. I got back up, my head pounding from the impact. I turned to Orpheus. The only emotion on his face was shock. His jaw dropped. His eyes were like planets; I could see the whites of his eyes perfectly. He pointed at the gears. "'ow the 'ell did you do that!?" he cried. I opened my mouth to ask him what, but when I turned back to the gears, my jaw dropped, too.

The gears were moving again.

I locked eyes with him, our expressions mirror images of each other. The only sound in the room now was the ticking of the gears. Several agonizingly long seconds went by before Orpheus finally spoke. "I ain't sayin' anythin'," he said.

"Ain't sayin' anythin'?" What the hell was that supposed to mean? I didn't want to talk about it. I quickly nodded and walked briskly out the door.

We walked in silence on the way back to the Lab. He didn't even look at me, which was both a blessing and a curse. Now I finally had the start of my answers.

What had happened that day at the riot was no coincidence. It really was me.

Ice cold fear gripped my soul. I knew that if anyone else caught me—anyone who was less kind and merciful as Orpheus—I would at best, be put in prison, and at worst, be put to death. Denying and suppressing my magic was only going to cause more trouble. Someone could get hurt, even killed, if this happened again. Orpheus' words echoed in my ears: *Magic is a living, breathing energy. But like anything in this world, it can be misused.* There really was now only one option.

If I'm going to have magic, I need to learn how to control it.

CHAPTER FIFTEEN

The rest of the day was very uneventful. I finished my training for the day, completely exhausted. My head ached, seeming to explode with all of the information I had learned. I tried to go over everything in my mind. My eyes struggled to stay open... I stumbled back to the bedroom...

But then I remembered what else happened today. I remembered the resolution I had come to. If I didn't start tonight, I'd keep putting it off until it was too late. A shot of adrenaline surged through me, awakening me. *Tonight.* I had to do it tonight.

But where could I practice without anyone seeing me? I thought about the great room I passed through with Orpheus; it was dark and secluded. No one could find me there. I shook my head. *That damned wall.* I couldn't think of any place I could go without being noticed; Darwin only knew the kind of security they had here.

Wait a minute. *Security.* I groaned inwardly. I knew where this was going. There was only one way to get what I wanted.

I saw Damon walking ahead of me, his face drooping with fatigue. I waited until everyone else passed before grabbing his shoulder and turning him towards me. "Hello, Damon," I said as seductively as I could. I could taste bile in my mouth. *It's just this one time,* I assured myself, cringing as I swallowed. *It'll be worth it.* "How was work today?"

His expression lit up with excitement and anticipation, leaving no trace of his previous exhaustion. "Everything was fine," he replied, his eyes conveying his insatiable want. I gulped, washing down another helping of bile. "How about you? How was your training?"

"I'm learning so much," I replied, shuddering as I traced my finger along the lines of his chest. "But it's so stressful, too. Is there a place where I—*we,* possibly—could be completely alone? No security, no cameras, nothing?"

A voracious smile slowly spread across Damon's face. My stomach churned, threatening to throw back up the beef I had for dinner. "Well, the only real place that has no security is in the bedrooms. But I'm sure you don't want everyone to hear us." I shuddered as I felt vomit rising up my throat like a volcano about to erupt.

"Exactly," I said, my voice straining.

"I guess the next best place would be the three rooms adjacent to the bedrooms," he replied. "Old labs from centuries ago. There's really nothing we can do with them now, so we just use them for storage. Just go through the door right next to the bedrooms." He stepped closer to me and placed his hands on my waist. "How about we go there tonight?"

I backed away from him, dizzy from nausea. "How about another night?" I asked. "Don't want to spoil a good thing."

Damon nodded. "Perfectly understandable," he replied. "Now, go to bed. We have a busy day tomorrow." He closed his eyes and leaned in for a kiss, his lips puckering like a fish. I hastily jogged away from him, leaving him standing awkwardly alone. I smiled to myself. *I guess I'm a better actress than I thought.*

But as I walked back to the bedroom in victory, I stopped. Wouldn't even storage rooms have locks? What if they stored valuable chemicals, or obscure elements or ancient books? As I walked towards the bedrooms, I shot a quick glance at the looming door standing across from the entrance. Looking around to make sure no one would see me, I snuck to the door. It was just... empty. No doorknob, no window into the next room. I pressed my body against it, pushing as hard as I could. It wouldn't budge. I skimmed over it with my fingers; maybe it was some kind of force field. Nothing happened. I examined the door carefully, studying its appearance, its texture. It didn't feel like any door I had ever encountered. As I was about to give up, I noticed a sleek clear panel next to the door. Thin white lines ran down and across the surface. *It looks just like my ArO-S.* A small indentation coursed down one side of it.

A key. I needed a key. But who would have the keys to a storage room? I went through the list of everyone I worked with. Charly and Aya weren't high up enough to be trusted with them. That left Orpheus, Damon, Dr. Vermaak, and Dr. Sharpe. I peeked into the bedrooms. Dr. Vermaak and Orpheus had already activated their force field walls, and there was no way in hell I was going to ask Aya for help. I thought of Dr. Sharpe; being the man in charge of the Project itself, surely he would have keys to the room. I shook my head, immediately dismissing the thought. *Nothing gets past him,* I thought. My stomach tied itself in knots. I had to get the keys from Damon. But how? *If I was an egotistic, creepy as hell pervert, where would I keep my keys?* A lump formed in my throat. The nausea that had relented earlier reared its ugly head once more. There was only one way to know.

I turned down the hall and saw Damon rounding the corner, his eyes downcast in embarrassment. I scanned the area around him, and saw a dark corner. I wanted to cry. I wanted to vomit. *Please let this cup pass over me.* As Damon walked closer to the bedrooms, I knew that my chance was slipping past me. I took a deep breath and braced myself as I walked hastily towards him.

"Hey," Damon said, his eyes darting up from the floor to me, "what are you—?"

I pinned him against the wall, silencing him with a violent kiss.

Damon's lips froze in surprise, but soon followed my lead. He inserted his slimy tongue into my mouth, swirling around inside it. My stomach heaved at the taste. Sure, he took care of himself, but the humiliation was almost too much to bear. *I'm giving this guy everything he wants.* Ice seemed to run across my skin, barely noticeable at first, but then colder, colder...

Shit. Not again!

His hands moved through my hair and down my body like worms—down my waist, over my backside, barely passing my womanhood until eventually sliding up my blouse and voraciously grabbing my breasts like a hungry animal. But past my shame, a single spark lit as I remembered the purpose of this charade. *It's only until you get the keys, Erin.*

I left his mouth, my soft kisses sliding down his jaw, his neck. Nausea consumed me as my hands roamed down his sides. I bit into his neck as I found the pockets of his lab coat. I shuddered as Damon moaned quietly. I fumbled around in one pocket. Nothing. I reached into another. Nothing in there, either. *Shit.* Desperate, I placed my hands on his chest, gently rubbing him as his hand wrapped around my hair. Just when I lost all hope, a square outline poked through the cloth, right into my hand. I opened my eyes as I reached inside and pulled out an ArO-S. *Bingo.* I quickly placed it into my own lab pocket and abruptly ended the kiss.

Damon traced his sweaty fingers down my cheek, eyes glazed with desire. "We'll have to continue this later, dear," he said gruffly.

I backed away. "We'll see," I said hurriedly as I ran to the bedrooms.

I found the nearest trash chute and vomited down it, the taste of beef, bile and stomach acid filling my mouth. My heaving echoed through the entire room. When I finished, I wiped my mouth with the sleeve of my blouse and started walking towards my bed before Charly stopped me. "Are you alright?" she asked softly. "You're not sick, are you?"

I nodded, but my lightheadedness made me regret it as I stumbled. She placed her hands on my shoulders to help keep me up. "I'm fine," I replied. "I'm just stressed. That and I think I had some bad beef."

Dr. Sharpe walked up behind her, his hands deep in his lab coat pockets. "Miss Chardonnay, what is going on?" he asked. He turned to me. "Miss Erin! Are you alright?"

"I'm fine," I replied, rubbing my eyes. "I promise. I just need to lie down."

"She certainly doesn't look fine, though," Charly interjected, her face wrinkled with concern.

"Thank you for your concern, Miss Chardonnay," Dr. Sharpe said. "But you should go and rest. Since my bed is closer to hers, I will escort Miss Erin."

I looked up at him, my eyebrows raised. "Y-you don't have to—"

"Not another word, Miss Erin," he said, his stern voice silencing my own. "You need your rest. I cannot have my newest recruit miss training for even a day." He wrapped his arm around my shoulder, guiding me to my bed.

"May I ask why you were seducing Dr. Ritter?" he inquired. "From how you have behaved around him the last few weeks, I assumed you loathed him with a fiery passion—possibly even feared him. Was my hypothesis incorrect?"

Shit. So he did see me. I couldn't tell him the real reason I was flirting with Damon. I sighed exasperatedly. *What the hell have I gotten myself into?* I looked back up to Dr. Sharpe, attempting to force my face to light up at the sound of his name.

"I guess my secret is out," I said, heaving as I felt the vomit rising once more. "The truth is that I flirt with him by teasing him. But I couldn't take it anymore; I had to tell him how I feel."

"Ah," Dr. Sharpe replied simply, frowning. "Personally, I discourage relationships among members of the Project," he continued. "If two people formed a relationship, but then it ended up failing, it would compromise the mission of the Project. I know you are still new to all of this, Miss Erin, but I would strongly advise you to be shrewd about pursuing relations with Dr. Ritter—or anyone else, for that matter."

"Don't worry," I said, rapidly nodding my head and sighing with relief. "I will."

"Good." We stopped as we approached my bed. "Now go to sleep. If you are still feeling ill in the morning, we can either give you medicine or have a Mage heal you."

I smiled. "I'm sure I'll be fine," I replied.

"Very well then." Dr. Sharpe walked slowly toward his bed. "Good night, everyone," he shouted. Quiet voices echoed through the hall like a hushed wind as they returned his farewell for the evening.

"Good night," I said, making doubly sure I remembered to form my wall *before* undressing. I set my lab coat on my hook, changed into a lavender silk nightgown and climbed into bed. I pulled the covers over me as the lights turned off. I held my breath and waited.

The noise faded, leaving behind nothing more than the ringing of deafening silence. I slowly climbed out of bed and moved the force field wall just enough for me to poke my head through.

The hall was completely empty. All of the force field walls were up.

Time to get to work, I thought as a burst of adrenaline shot through my veins.

I walked over to my lab coat and pulled Damon's ArO-S out of the pocket. I tiptoed out of my bedroom, shuddering at the chill of the marble floor. I turned and closed the wall and walked as briskly and silently as I could down the hall.

"No! No!"

I froze as Damon's voice rang through the room. *Shit.* I clutched the ArO-S to my chest, hiding it from view. I waited fearfully for Damon's wall to open, for him to chastise me, to find the ArO-S and rip it from my grasp. Or worse…

"Please no, Emily!" he cried again, this time more distressed.

Emily? I frowned. *Who the hell is Emily?* I shook my head. *I don't have time for this,* I thought as I continued down the room.

I stopped at the massive door and checked my surroundings. *I'm still alone,* I thought, sighing with relief. But even with this realization, my body was still tense. I stared at the door. *Please don't make noise,* I pleaded with it. I pushed the door open as gently as I could. *So far, so good.* I drew in a sharp breath and bit my lip; the door creaked like old bones. I looked around again, but couldn't hear any shuffling. *Damn, these people are heavy sleepers.* Even so, the noise echoed through the silence like a bomb. I moved the door enough to wear I could squeeze my body through it. As I pulled it shut I laughed to myself, relieved. *That was almost too easy.*

I focused my attention on the empty entrance in front of me. I flinched as I released my death grip on the ArO-S. The sharp edges had pierced my skin, and droplets of blood ran down my flesh like tears. Sighing, I wiped my hand on the skirt of my nightgown and walked closer to the door. I eyed the panel on the wall. Hesitantly, I grabbed the ArO-S and ran it down the gap.

"Welcome, Dr. Damon Ritter," the same womanly voice echoed through the hall. The door slid open, revealing a dark room. *Well, that was easy,* I thought as I stepped inside.

Darkness filled the entire room. I coughed violently as the smell of dust, musty old books and lab equipment filled my nostrils. The blackness consumed everything as the door shut behind me. "A light," I said aloud to myself. "Where's a light?" I slid my finger down the ArO-S, the holographic menu providing a dim glow. I skimmed my hands along the wall, hoping to find at least some sort of switch. *If I'm going to practice magic, I want to be able to see what I'm doing.* My hand found a small panel near the door, similar to the one outside. A series of smaller indentations ran up the device, just large enough to fit two fingers in them. I delicately placed two fingers in the depressions, the room lighting up as I slid them.

Nothing but boxes upon boxes filled the room, blocking the glory of the faded paintings. I barely could take two steps forward without tripping over something. "I'm going to need more room than this," I said. Sighing in exasperation, I knelt down and attempted to pick up a box filled with ancient spell books. *They really need to take better care of these artifacts,* I thought, shaking my head. *These spell books are priceless. Darwin only knows how old they are.* My body ached as I lifted the crate. "Why are these books so damned heavy?" I placed the crate of spell books on top of a box of old lab equipment. *They may be able to help me,* I thought, making a mental note to keep them around for future reference.

Lifting that one box alone took a lot of energy from me, but it still didn't leave me much room. *I don't have time to move boxes. Exhaustion may affect my magic... maybe?* Was that how magic worked? *I'll find out. I'm here to learn.* I sat down in the small circle I had made by moving the box of books and crossed my legs, placing my hands on my knees. I closed my eyes and took several deep breaths. *Is this how I do it?* I thought, thinking back to when Orpheus used his magic. But he was able to summon it with ease, as if it were second nature, without having to sit and meditate. *He's a Mage, idiot,* I thought to myself, shaking my head at my utter stupidity. I continued to take deep, even breaths, my heart rate beating steadily like a metronome. I could feel the natural rhythm of my body as I meditated. *Boom, ba-boom, ba-boom...* I cleared my head of all intruding thoughts: Damon, Dr. Sharpe, the Gears, even the longing to see my parents again. I became lighter, my soul seeming to leave my body as I felt a rumbling hum rising from the earth, moving through my legs, up my body and into my head. The same energy that shot through my veins that day in New Washington ran through me once again. Only this time, it wasn't like raging rapids... it was peaceful, like a river. The steady stream didn't frighten me. If anything, it calmed me. I smiled, welcoming it as an old friend. By instinct, I lifted my hand, my eyes still closed, and breathed deeply as the warm energy flowed through my arm into my right hand. The warmth left my body, but I could still feel its pulse beating in my palm and between my fingers; I was holding the heart of the earth. Opening my eyes, adrenaline shot through my veins.

My hand was on fire!

"Son of a bitch!" I shouted, waving my hand violently to put out the flames. As I shook my hand, the fire left my palm and flew through the air. *Shit, I'm going to end up burning this place to the ground!* I bit my lip anxiously as the ball of fire flew towards a group of boxes ahead of me. I sighed in relief as the weak flames burned out before damaging the artifacts.

I shook my head. "Erin, you idiot," I chastised myself. *Oh, well,* I thought. *This is why I'm practicing.* But still, if I couldn't even control a simple flame, how was I going to break the laws of nature and walk through a solid object? I sighed.

"I have a lot of work to do."

CHAPTER SIXTEEN

"Can I say something, Erin?" Dr. Vermaak asked.

Her voice startled me, the shot of adrenaline waking me back up. I had stayed up most of the night in the storage room, but at the cost of my energy and focus for today. I could feel Dr. Sharpe's icy stare boring into my back, disappointed in what he called my "lack of discipline and discretion." He left me to my own devices, giving me the job of calculating several series of difficult physics equations. *I thought I'd be done with homework once I left school,* I thought, rolling my eyes and shaking my head.

"Erin?" Dr. Vermaak asked again.

I drew in a sharp breath and rubbed my eyes. "Yes?"

"I don't know what it is," she replied, "but you seem a lot calmer than usual today." Her eyebrows furrowed. "Then again, maybe it's just because you're tired. Is everything alright?"

I yawned. "Yeah, yeah, I'm fine. Just a rough night is all."

Her concerned expression never left her face. "Alright," she said, her eyes piercing mine. "Just make sure you get some rest. It's not healthy to neglect sleep." She started to walk away, but turned back to me. "You do know you can tell me anything, right?" she asked. "I know I seem harsh, but I genuinely care about you. You and everyone here."

I nodded. "Thanks," I said, a small smile crossing my face. "But I'm fine. I promise."

Dr. Vermaak nodded slowly. "Alright," she said. "I'm going to ask about the Mages' progress. But that offer still stands." And with that she walked away.

I brought my attention back to the equations before me. *Okay, so if the engine is spinning at a rate of...*

"'ey, Damon!" Orpheus shouted. Turning around, I saw Damon slowly walk in, his shoulders slumped. Dark bags sat under his weary eyes, his hair an uneven mess.

Orpheus frowned. "You don't look so good, Damon," he said. "Is everything alright?"

He slowly lifted his eyes to Orpheus, as if it took all of his energy to meet the Mage's gaze. "Yeah, I'm fine," he replied as he nodded. "Everything's fine. Just couldn't sleep is all."

I raised an eyebrow. *Where's the complacency? I mean, I'm not complaining, but still...* Could this have something to do with "Emily?" I thought back to the previous evening. The pain in his voice stabbed me like an ice pick, his voice breaking like shattering glass. *Damon may be an arrogant son of a bitch,* I thought. *But I'm not heartless enough to revel in his pain.*

"I hope you will be able to focus, Dr. Ritter," Dr. Sharpe said. "We cannot afford to have the mission compromised."

"Yes, sir," Damon sighed as he sluggishly walked to an empty terminal. As he passed me, I grabbed his arm.

"What's going on?"

He shook his arm from my grasp. "I don't have time for this," he said. The same pain from last night still emanated from his voice, the solemn bells of a funeral march. "We have a lot of work to do today."

My mouth dropped open. My voice was gone. *Damn, this must be bad.*

"Miss Erin!" Dr. Sharpe shouted, startling me. "I need those equations!"

"Yes, sir!" I squeaked, turning my attention back to the equations in front of me.

Charly walked over to me. "Do you know what's wrong with Dr. Ritter?" she asked, concern reflected in her eyes.

"Damon?" I shrugged. "I don't know. He always just tried to make feeble advances. I've never seen him like this, though."

Charly frowned. "You're hiding something," she said, staring into my eyes. "You know something, and you're not telling me."

I raised an eyebrow. "Hiding something?" I asked. "Why would I have a reason to hide anything?"

"Embarrassment," she replied, maintaining eye contact with me. Her stern gaze wouldn't let me go until she got an answer. "Guilt," she continued. "What happened last night wasn't illness; you've done something to him."

Heat rose up to my cheeks. My hands clenched into fists. *Shit. I've got to run away.*

"We can't fix this until I know what happened," Charly pressed.

I stood frozen, feeling the temperature dropping every second. *Not again...*

Charly's frown vanished. Genuine concern radiated from her face. She slowly reached for my hands and gently unfurled them. Warmth flowed from her hands into mine, running up and down my body. The chill dissipated. My body relaxed. I took a deep breath, allowing the warmth to consume me.

"There," she said, releasing my hands. "Are you alright now?"

120

"Much better," I replied, giving her a small smile.

"Good," she said, grinning in return. "Now, can you tell me what happened?"

I sighed in defeat. "I... I kissed him," I said, blushing. "Last night. On the way back to the bedrooms."

Charly's jaw dropped. "I thought you said you hated him!" she cried, her voice bitten by shock.

"I do!" I shouted, flinching as my voice echoed through the laboratory. I quickly looked around, hoping no one had heard me. When I was sure that no one was paying attention, I continued. "Why do you think I vomited?" I whispered. "It's not like I enjoyed it."

Charly raised an eyebrow. "Then what reason would you have to kiss him?"

I opened my mouth, but caught myself before I said anything incriminating. "I can't tell you."

Her lips pursed into a fine line. "Well, you just tell me when you're ready," she said. She placed her hand on my shoulder. "It's like I said before. We're in this together. I can't force you to say anything. But please know that if you ever need anything, you can come to any of us."

"But not Dr. Sharpe or Aya," I chuckled.

"Dr. Sharpe may seem stern and unfeeling," Charly replied, "but that's just him trying to be professional. His aura says more... *a lot* more." She ran her fingers through her fiery red hair. "But I don't know what's going on with Aya," she continued. "She's been tense and cold to everyone ever since Dr. Sharpe left for New Washington. I can talk to her, if you want."

I shook my head. "No, thanks. I can deal with it."

Charly nodded. "Okay." She threw her arms around me.

The foreign touch startled me. The softness of her words, the refuge in her arms... Mother would often hug me, but it had been so long since I felt that sense of security I had almost forgotten what it felt like to be loved. Her head rested on my shoulders, her arms wrapped around me like a safety net. I swallowed, fighting the lump that was beginning to form in my throat. But as Charly squeezed me tighter, I lost control as the tears fell down my face, their salt stinging my eyes. I laughed at myself. *How many times have you cried now?* My arms in turn wrapped around her, gripping her robes as my body rocked to the rhythm of my sobs. But as the tears flowed and landed on Charly's green and purple robes, waves of catharsis rolled over me, and my weeping became a much needed storm after a long drought.

Charly stepped back, wiping my tears with her hands. "Please don't be afraid," she said. "As generic as this is going to sound, I know that you're going to do great things. You are capable of so much more than you realize. There's a reason why Dr. Sharpe chose you out of everyone in New Washington, let alone New Pangaea. He sees greatness in you. I see greatness in you. Orpheus and Vynessa see greatness in you. I'm pretty sure even Damon and Aya see greatness in you. If you could only learn to see that greatness in yourself; you could become the greatest Chemist the Golgotha Project—and New Pangaea—has ever seen."

Her words struck me like lightning. *Don't be afraid. Be not afraid.* "Those words have been following me around a lot lately," I said with a smirk.

"Because they're true," Charly answered. "If there's one thing I've learned about you after all the time you've been here, it's that you have the tendency to be afraid. To fear that you'll be a disappointment. To doubt the power that you have." She took my hands again. "These hands are capable of so much more than you can imagine. Use them to bring healing, to make New Pangaea even better than it is now. All of us—myself included—know that you can do it."

I nodded. "Thanks, Charly," I said, blushing at her kind words. "I really needed that." I gave her a small, crooked smile. "I guess your prediction was right," I added. "I think we are going to be great friends."

"Of course!" Charly replied with a laugh. "My predictions are never wrong!" I giggled as the last of my worries slipped away. "Well, Dr. Vermaak's coming back over. You might want to get back to those equations." She started to walk away once again. "By the way, before you ask, reading auras takes practice. A lot of practice." She skipped back towards Orpheus, her robes flying behind her on a gentle breeze.

Be not afraid. I brought my hair back behind my ears. *Easier said than done.* But still, that message echoed in my brain, a faint light in a dark cavern. I had so many expectations put on me. Was my magic failing me? Was it only hurting me?

Wait...

I looked around, making sure that everyone was occupied in their own research. I brought my sleeves up and looked at my arms.

Both of my hands were scarred by second degree burns. Long scars ran up my arms. I checked my neck, feeling the familiar smoothness of scar tissue. I examined their shapes, the way they coursed down my body like vines.

My magic was leaving me physically disfigured.

Why would it do that to me? How could Mages possess such power and wield it without any damage to them at all? Were my parents right? Was it truly unnatural for a Chemist to dabble in magic? For a Mage to learn science? Was this a consequence of my actions? I never chose to have magic. If I had it my way, I never would have chosen it in the first place. But everyone is born the way they are, and sometimes the way we're born can be different, even downright frightening. But rather than fight it, one should come to terms with it, and do the best they can. After all, I was always taught to question everything. I never saw the harm that came from magic. I had seen magic do beautiful, wonderful things during my time here at the Project. I had seen science do beautiful, wonderful things, too. But I also saw the darkness each side was capable of. Images of the riot that day in New Washington flashed through my mind. I flinched at the dead bodies, the blood that watered the city's streets. I had seen nothing but hatred in the eyes of both Mages and Chemists. The resolution I had made to myself yesterday didn't fade, even after seeing the scars. If anything, it made that feeling stronger. I needed more than all-night practice sessions in that dark, lonely storage room. I needed to focus all of my energy on it—without disrupting my scientific research, of course. I took a deep breath and closed my eyes, repeating the same process of meditation. *Ba-boom, ba-boom, ba-boom…* The heart of the earth pulsed through me, meshing perfectly with my own heartbeat like the cogs of a gear. As I opened my eyes, a calm focus washed over me. A path to the answers opened before me, both to the equations and to my future. I turned my focus to the work Dr. Sharpe gave me.

For the first time in my life, I was confident in my work.

CHAPTER SEVENTEEN

"And then I said, 'I swear, the next time I 'ear someone say 'your' instead of 'you're,' I'm gonna split a 'ole in *them!*'"

The entire table roared with laughter as we dined. Bits of turkey flew out of Orpheus' mouth as he laughed and told his story. "That shut 'im up real quick," Orpheus continued as he swallowed another bite of his turkey leg. "I'm not sure if 'e'll let me buy elements from 'im now, though."

"I see your logic, Mr. Brown," Dr. Sharpe said with a chuckle.

I giggled in concert with him. I hadn't taken the time to notice it before, but it was always adorable to see Dr. Sharpe, a strict, stern man, attempt to convey humor. While he didn't laugh outright, his small smile lit up his eyes, the one key to his inner self...

I shook my head, catching myself at the thoughts that ran through my mind. *What the hell is wrong with me?* I always had a sense of respect for him, nothing more. But the more I practiced my magic, the more in tune I became with my emotions. But this feeling... I had never felt it before... The question echoed through my mind over and over again. My heart pumped faster and faster... anxiety once again ran through me like an arctic river... but it wasn't the same... maybe, just maybe... could I read my own aura?

I wonder... I closed my eyes and took a deep breath, calling on the heart of the earth to beat through me once again. *Ba-boom... ba-boom...* As I opened my eyes, the entire room was washed in grey. A rainbow of colors, some that I had never even seen before, surrounded each person. A million different shades of orange radiated from Orpheus as he laughed, reflecting his inner social and comedic self. Charly's aura pulsed with happy, gregarious, pink and blue sparks, her body bouncing as she giggled. Motherly shades of green surrounded Dr. Vermaak as she stared around the room, smiling as she observed the camaraderie amongst her co-workers and friends.

But it was Dr. Sharpe's aura that confused me the most. Logical yellow pulsed through it, but so did a mixture of brown and black... *what the hell does that mean?* I had never seen brown and black before. *Why can't I understand what that means?* Maybe I just didn't have enough experience? As he turned to look at me, his aura began to pulse faster and faster. The colors swirled around him like a hurricane. His eyes radiated confusion and... heat? I looked away as the normal colors of the room replaced the grey.

"Erin," Dr. Vermaak said, placing her hand on mine. "You don't look so good."

I nodded quickly. "Yeah, I'm fine," I replied. "Just a slight headache, that's all."

"Eat something, then!" Orpheus said, his mouth filled with beans. He pointed to my nearly full plate. "You haven't touched your food all night! If you don't want it, I'll be happy to take it."

I smiled weakly. "Sure," I replied.

Dr. Sharpe stood up, abruptly. "It is getting late," he said, his commanding voice echoing through the room.

"As always, thank you all for a profitable day of research. You truly are a blessing to New Pangaea."

Everyone else got up out of their chairs and proceeded to walk down the hallway towards the bedrooms. Exhaustion hung over me like a veil over my eyes; the room seemed foggy. Everything seemed to be melting around me. But my brain couldn't process the idea of sleep.

"Aren't you coming to bed, Erin?" Dr. Vermaak asked, her eyebrows furrowing.

I looked up at her. "In a little bit," I replied as I stood up. "I still have some work to do. I should be done in half an hour."

"Are you sure that's smart?" she returned. "You look exhausted. I'm glad you've been so calm lately, but if it's because you're not sleeping, that's not healthy. You need your rest."

I smiled. "I will; don't worry."

She nodded. "Okay," she said. "Have a good night." She followed the others down the hall.

I stood up and started walking back to the main lab. I wasn't lying; Dr. Sharpe was just giving me more equations and problems to solve. Ever since that first day I practiced magic, all he had done was doubt me. I remembered Charly's words, but I still found them hard to believe. Still… the way his aura pulsed when he looked at me… his hard, intimidating expression…

"Hello, lovely."

I stopped dead in my tracks and inwardly groaned. *Son of a bitch.*

I turned around, and there Damon stood, staring me down with his lustful eyes.

"What are you doing here?" I asked.

"What am I doing here?" he retorted, his voice oozing with desire. I tried to back away, but before I could even take a step Damon had grabbed my wrists and pinned me against the cold stone wall.

"Get off of me!" I shouted, squirming in his iron grasp.

"What for?" he asked. "As I recall, *you* were the one who first kissed *me*. Don't deny yourself... I know you want to...."

"I didn't do it for you!" I snapped. "But I had to!"

Damon frowned, but the hunger in his eyes didn't fade. "What do you mean 'you had to?'"

"There's no chance in *hell* I'm telling you! You think I want to risk my ass for *you*?"

His eyebrows furrowed. The ferocity of his gaze subsided, replaced by the natural, quizzical nature of a Chemist, but he still didn't let me go. The gears in his head spun as he processed this information. He released one hand, reached into my lab pocket and pulled out his ArO-S.

My eyes widened. I stopped squirming. *Shit.*

"Dr. Vermaak has been letting me use her key for the past four weeks. Everything had been moved. There were marks on the wall, too. Marks that can only be made by magic..." I winced as he moved the cloth up my arm, scraping my still sensitive skin.

"Burn marks..." he whispered to himself. He looked back up at me, his blue eyes churning with rage. "Damn it, Erin!" he screamed. "You're using magic, aren't you!?"

"Shhh!" I tried to cover his mouth with my hand. "I don't want anyone to know."

He slapped my hand away. "What the hell are you thinking!?" he screamed, his voice bouncing off the walls. I cowered slightly. "Do you even know what you're doing? There are severe consequences for things like this! What if Dr. Sharpe found out? The rest of the Project? The Supreme Leader? Your parents? You know what will happen? At best, they'll blackball you from ever receiving a specialization, and you'll be doomed to a life of poverty! At worst, they'll put you to death!"

"They can put me to death!" I screamed, tears welling up in my eyes. "I never chose this! You really think I'd choose something that would put my life and my family at risk!?"

"I'm not saying you chose anything!" Damon shrieked, his contorted face a pulsing blood red. "I'm saying that the last thing I want is to see you get hurt!"

"What the hell do you care!? I'm nothing more than a sex toy to you!"

He threw his hands up in the air. "Damn it, Emily!"

We froze. Not even the sound of our breathing echoed through the cavernous halls. The blood in Damon's face vanished as it turned into a sickly pale white. My heart pounded. The temperature rose around me. There it was again. That name.

"Who's Emily?"

Damon swallowed, his haunted eyes averting my gaze. He quickly turned and ran away, his white lab coat trailing behind him, tears running down his cheeks.

I turned around and walked slowly towards the lab, shocked by what had just happened. But the same questions ran through my head. *Who is Emily? And why would Damon call me that?* Maybe this was the opportunity I had been waiting for. Whoever this Emily was, she was obviously a source of misery for Damon. If I reminded him so much of her, he would finally leave me alone! I would be free! But my footsteps slowed as I remembered the cries of agony I had heard that night, the misery in his voice. I could almost feel the tears running down his face, the knife of heartbreak stabbing into him over and over again. Even a jerk like Damon didn't deserve this. I sighed. *Damn it all.* I turned around and quickly ran after him.

Where is he? I ran through the painted halls until I reached the foyer. *I haven't lost him, have I?* I desperately looked around, hoping to find the familiar blond hair and white lab coat. I took a deep breath. *You won't be able to find him unless you're calm.*

"Find Emily." Damon's voice echoed through the hall straight ahead of me. A white and blond mass sat hunched in a corner, the dark corridor lit up by the light of his ArO-S. I slowly walked towards him, my footsteps faintly echoing. But as I neared him and sat down, I drew in a sharp breath.

We were at the wall.

"Her name was Emily," Damon said quietly. "Emily DeRayne. Several years ago, she was part of the Golgotha Project as a Chemist, studying mechanical engineering. She was the smartest, sweetest woman I ever knew. She never stopped learning, never stopped asking questions." He cleared his throat. "And she was so beautiful. I was so desperately in love with her. I admired everything about her: her eyes, her smile, the way she would snort when she laughed. She was the reason I woke up every day. She was the reason I wanted to become not only a better Chemist, but a better person all around."

I sat down next to him. *Never thought I'd do something like this out of my own free will.* I pushed aside my opinions on Damon and hesitantly put a hand on his shoulder. "So what happened?" I asked.

He sighed. "She was almost too curious. It was while she was here she discovered her magical capabilities. She confided in me one day after everyone else had gone to bed that she had been secretly practicing magic in one of the smaller labs. She showed me the scars that ran up her legs and down her arms; it was like her blood was on fire and had scarred her from the inside out.

She showed me this wall that night, too. She was sure that there was something behind this wall. She didn't know what, but she could tell that something wasn't right." He rubbed his eyes. "I should've said something to her. I should've said that she needed to forget about the magic, forget about the wall. I should've told her how much I loved her, and that I didn't want to see her get hurt." He laughed morbidly at himself. "I was a coward. I was so afraid a woman like her would never fall for a man like me. But by the time I gathered up the courage to tell her how I really felt, it was too late. She was found dead the next morning in the very same room she practiced in."

"The storage room I've been using?"

He nodded, sniffling as he wiped his eyes. "I couldn't stand to set foot in there. I couldn't even stand to look at the door to it. I asked Dr. Sharpe if we could just move everything into the main ballroom, and he said yes. Dr. Sharpe may seem cold, but he really is empathetic. I think he understood where I was coming from."

A light bulb seemed to go off in my head. "That's why that first night you told me about the storage room, I heard you crying out her name. I had never heard so much pain in one voice in my life."

"In my dream, Emily was in the room, practicing her magic, and I was in there. She turned around and lit herself on fire with her magic. I tried to stop her, but she turned to ashes before I could even utter her name." He broke down in tears, his sobs echoing throughout the corridor. "They sent me to New Washington five years ago to get over her death. And that's where I met you. You remind me so much of her, Erin. Your inquisitive nature, the way your eyes light up when you figure out an answer to a question. Your hair, your eyes. If reincarnation was possible, I would swear you were Emily returning to me."

I wiped my eyes, too proud to admit that Damon, the man I claimed to hate, brought sympathetic tears to my eyes.

He handed me his ArO-S. "This is what she looks like."

Chestnut hair fell down to her shoulders like waves of the ocean. Her round face lit up with her small, pink smile. Even in the stillness of the photograph, her emerald eyes seemed to burn with life. *Wow. She really does look like me.* "She's beautiful," I said.

"Yes," Damon replied. "I still think about her every day."

I bit my lip, almost too reluctant to ask. I pointed to the wall ahead of me. "Is there anything behind that wall?"

Damon shrugged. "To be honest, I don't know. No one knows. It's been there for as long as I can remember." He cupped one hand around my cheek. "I know you're curious. But please. This wall only brings pain and death. I can't lose you."

I sighed, taking Damon's hand in my own. "I know you're scared, Damon," I said, shocked by the sweetness of my voice. "But for the past few months, I've been learning to control my magic. I'll be okay. I promise." I gripped his hand tighter. "Just please," I said. "I'm begging you. Don't tell anyone. I'd rather die by magic than be executed by the state."

He brought me close to him, his hold not lustful or angry... but full of sorrow. I froze, his emotional intimacy catching me by surprise. "I love you. Please. Be careful."

"I will," I replied.

I froze again as he placed a gentle kiss on my forehead. "I'm going to bed. Good night, Em... Erin." He stood up and walked away slowly, his red face still stained with tears.

Well damn, I thought as I sat on that cold marble floor. *Don't I feel like a bitch.* All this time, I had treated Damon like he was nothing more than an arrogant piece of shit. But there was so much more than that. *Emily.* She was just like me. A mere Chemist with incredible abilities. Abilities that brought her to her death. Fear chilled my soul. Was I to share her fate? Was all of this worth the risk? I thought back to that day in the clock tower, when I restored the Headquarters' power with just my hands. I remembered what Charly said to me the next day. *These hands are capable of so much more than you can imagine.*

I had to know what rested beyond this wall. Emily must have been on to something. Regardless of what else lay before me, I had to take this risk. Resolve swelled within me. Enough with the practicing.

Tonight is the night.

CHAPTER EIGHTEEN

I crawled over to the wall until my nose touched its surface An unfamiliar smell filled my nostrils. *Mold? Dust?* I coughed into my arm, gagging at the rotten stench. I quickly shook my head, trying to bring back the focus I had. *Come on, Erin. Focus. Breathe.* I crossed my legs, resting my hands on my knees. I closed my eyes and tuned out everything around me: the hum of the lights, the icy cold marble on my skin, even the foul smell that violated my senses. The sound of my heartbeat was the only thing that mattered at this point. It pulsed through my chest like a metronome, keeping the rest of my body in rhythm. I could hear the blood rushing through my veins like rivers. Even my thoughts were silenced.

And there it was. The heart of the earth, beating in the ground under me like a loud timpani. My heart slowed until they both began to move in time. I was no longer Erin; I was part of the earth. The familiar oneness and peace took over me as the connection between myself and the earth grew stronger, her arms open and willing to embrace me.

I want to move beyond this wall, I thought, my voice reverberating inside my head.

The heartbeats sped up, creating a heat that radiated from my chest. The heat traveled from my chest, down my arms and into my hands. I lifted my hands slowly as invisible sparks fell from my fingers. I opened my eyes and quickly pressed my hands against the wall. The energy left my hands and went into it. I sat in apprehension, waiting for something to happen: an explosion, a disappearing act, anything.

Nothing.

I dropped my head, disappointed and agitated. Maybe I didn't practice enough. Maybe I didn't do it correctly. Maybe it just wasn't meant to be. I sighed. Damon was probably right. I was already going to get into a lot of trouble already. I should probably just drop it. I have it controlled enough to where I won't cause any accidents again, anyway. Wasn't that my goal in the first place? I stood up and rubbed my eyes, fighting back tears of frustration. I started heading down the corridor to go back to bed and put this magic mess behind me.

A low rumbling stopped me dead in my tracks.

I slowly turned around, my eyes widening in shock. The rumbling continued, pulsating through my feet and up my body. The wall radiated a white and gold aura, the lights brighter around the edges of each brick. *What the hell?* I stepped closer, staring as the wall began to part down the middle, each brick sliding on top of the one next to it until it created a small dark hole just large enough for one person to fit through.

I stood there in awe. A huge smile ran across my face, and I jumped in the air as I pumped my fists. *I finally did it!* I knew there was something there! If it really was just a back wall, it would have opened up to the river behind the Headquarters. It was already night, but even the light of the moon and the Gears would have illuminated the land enough for one to make out the silhouette of a river. But as the wall opened up, the stench I had encountered moments ago grew ten times—no, a *hundred* times—stronger.

Whatever is back here is one of two things: ancient or damning. Maybe both.

I reached down to the edge of my lab coat and easily tore off a strip of cloth from the bottom, my hands still burning from the magic. I winced as the coarse material scratched my singed skin. *Shit. I forgot about that part.* I wrapped the cloth around my nose and mouth, and crawled into the hole.

The light from the hall behind me gave only enough light to illuminate a few feet of the path. I took a deep breath and held up my hand. The heart of the earth beat through me again as a faint ball of light formed above my hand. I stared straight ahead. "Well... here goes," I said to myself.

The place beyond the barricade was nothing more than another, more barren corridor. But if there was one thing I had learned over these past few months, it was to never underestimate anything. Despite the disappointing appearance of the deserted hall, I trudged forward.

Mold and dust filled my nostrils, causing me to sneeze for Darwin only knows how long. I cringed as I felt old mud seep in through my shoes. Cobwebs hung from the ceiling. Empty canvases lined the walls, faded after hundreds of years of neglect.

Squeak!

I quickly covered my mouth, trying to hold back a scream. *Someone caught me!* I quickly turned around, but saw nothing. In my peripheral vision, I caught sight of a black mass scurrying around. I moved the light towards the mass, and sighed in relief. *It's just a rat.* I laughed at myself. *Some things never change.*

I continued walking forward, dodging the mud puddles, my eyes also constantly scanning the floor for more rats. *This place must have been beautiful a thousand years ago,* I mused. *I wonder what this place was used for—*

I crashed into a back wall.

I grabbed my face, my nose aching as if someone had ran a car right into it. "Ahh! Damn it!" I looked up. A dusty old wall sat in front of me. *Oh, come on! Another wall?* But the walls around me didn't reflect any of my light.

In fact, there weren't any walls at all.

There were two different hallways, all lined with doors. I chuckled in satisfaction. *Bingo.* But which way should I go? It would take all night to explore this forgotten wing, and I had to be at the bedrooms by at least 6:00, so no one would suspect anything. *I can choose a random door, I guess,* I thought to myself. I looked around, trying to make a decision. All of the doors looked the same. I used my free hand to open my ArO-S. *11:00 p.m.* Seven hours. I removed the cloth and coughed, dizzy from breathing in carbon dioxide, before quickly replacing it. *Darwin only knows what kind of bacteria and diseases have taken refuge here.*

As I continued to ponder which way to go, I found myself drawn to a particular door on my left. It seemed old and ordinary, like any other door here. But there was something about it... as if it was beckoning me... "Oh, what the hell?" I walked to the door. The rotted wood hung in front of me like an old corpse. The door buckled and creaked as I moved the doorknob. I jumped back as the wood bowed and collapsed, leaving an empty hole. My heavy breathing echoed through the corridor. Fear and panic welled up within me. *You've come this far, Erin,* I thought. *It's just one more door.* I gulped and slowly walked through the opening.

But as I entered, my jaw dropped. My light nearly went out.

"I've found you."

There were books everywhere. On old tables, on mountainous shelves, they rested, untouched for millennia. Some were even opened to pages of dead languages I could never hope to understand. And they weren't the books that one could easily download onto an ArO-S. They were true books, bound together by cloth and leather, the letters printed in ink as dark as the night. I didn't even mind the stench that bled through my makeshift mask. These were the most prized ancient artifacts. I could have spent an eternity in this darkness, caught up in the tales of old, the days when my father's car was considered state of the art. But one question still plagued my thoughts.

"What could be in here that's so bad someone would want to lock it away?"

I walked around the room, attempting to make sense of the language in the books. Old proverbs and quotes lined the pages of the tomes. Titles of the works rested sideways on the spines of the books on the shelves. I kept moving, desperately wanting to understand the world before New Pangaea...

Golgotha.

The familiar word stopped me in my tracks. I took a few steps back and held up the light to the word. It was on the spine of an old blue book.

The Gears of Golgotha.

The title attracted my curiosity. *Why would they want to hide away the origins of the Project?* I held my breath as I delicately pulled the thick book out of its shelf with my finger. The pages didn't disintegrate. The words of wisdom were still there. I ran to the nearest table, stacked the other books that occupied it into piles and gently laid down the great work.

The title, bound in blue leather, was written in faded gold letters, accompanied by the same two gears as the ones on New Pangaea's flag. I opened it, and smiled when I saw the text. *English.* A sense of awe washed over me. *I can't believe I'm actually reading a thousand year old text about our nation!* I placed my finger on one paragraph and started reading.

This project, hereafter referred to as Golgotha, I began, giddy, *shall be the salvation of a world broken by war for the third time. Using kinetic energy, the Gears shall be placed alongside our moon as satellites, ever moving due to the magnetic field that powers their core.* A sketch of the Gears was drawn below the text, as well as what appeared to be a small blue sun in the center. *The energy they provide shall be enough power to restore society to its former glory.*

However, even this revolutionary concept does not completely solve the problems of our world.

I frowned. *What do they mean?*

The Gears' production of energy is finite. If they are overworked, they shall short-circuit, and stop moving.

I stopped and closed the book. "That must be why there have been so many power outages lately!" I said to myself. "We're using too much energy!" I closed the book and started to run towards the door. "I've got to tell Dr. Sharpe—!"

My foot struck something, and I fell to the floor.

Dirt covered my face, stinging my eyes. I removed the cloth and attempted to clean myself. "What the—?" I froze, my eyes widening in fear.

I had tripped over and fallen on top of a skeleton.

I screamed. "What the hell!?" I looked next to it, and there lay another skeleton.

My light went out. "Shit!" I brought my hand up and tried desperately to make another orb, but with no luck. I groaned and dug around in my pocket, sighing in relief as I felt the familiar square smoothness of my ArO-S. I brought it out and slid my finger across it. The light of the menu created just enough light for me to see the bodies below me.

The one I had landed on had been crushed, reduced to nothing more than a pile of ashes. Another smaller skeleton laid next to it. I looked closer. A faded lab coat rested in the ashes, stained by death and neglect. The smaller skeleton wore a lab coat, but what appeared to be a Mage's robe was folded underneath it. I knelt down and dusted off the ashes. But when I saw what was buried under them, I screamed.

The name *T. Luciani* was embroidered on the pocket.

I quickly checked the other pocket. *E. Luciani.*

Tom and Evelyn Luciani.

"Mother! Father!"

I bolted out the entrance as fast as I could. I didn't even try to control my sobbing; my cries echoed through the cavernous ruins. I didn't care if I woke up all of London; I just wanted to go home. If those two skeletons really were Tom and Evelyn Luciani, then who are my mother and father? Who was I? *Please, Darwin, please let this be a nightmare! I want to wake up to my Mother and Father. I want to finally be able to eat that cake. I don't want to have magic.* I ran and ran, not caring what or where I had to pass through to get home. I didn't even notice that I had reached the lit part of Headquarters.

I stopped and folded my hands on my head, trying desperately to catch my breath. Tears and sweat rolled down my face. I winced, trying to ignore the pain in my heart, my head, my chest. "This pain isn't worth it!" I bawled, throwing down my lab coat.

"Erin—?"

I wiped my eyes and looked up. There she was. The last person I wanted to see.

Aya.

My jaw dropped as my brain processed what was really happening. The wall was opened. My hands were scarred by magic. My face was blood red and swollen from my cries. My lab coat was on the ground.

There was no way I could hide it any longer. She knew.

I shot up and sped past her so quickly my tears fell behind me. *I have to get out of here.*

"Erin, wait!" Aya shouted.

I ignored her pleas and shot straight down the hall, not stopping for anything, even for breathing. Blood pumped through me as I pushed my body to its boundaries. My head throbbed with blood and adrenaline as I kept running and running and running...

The cold night air cut through me as I pushed open the last door. Rain poured down on London's streets in buckets, drenching me as soon as I took that first step. My tears and sweat mixed with the tears of the earth.

"Please, Darwin!" I begged. "Take this away from me!" I fell to the ground, vomiting, my howls and wails muted by the roar of the rain.

I sat there wrapped in my agony for what felt like an eternity. As I wiped the tears and rain from my face, a black figure moved in from the shadows. I frowned. *Who would be out this late?* The streetlights shone down on him.

A Silent One.

I stood up and brought my hair back. "Sorry about that, sir," I shouted. Nothing about his face changed. He just stood there, a statue in a wax museum. "I had a horrible nightmare. I just needed some fresh night air to calm myself down. I'm better now, though." I pointed to the door, smiling awkwardly. "I'm going to go back to bed now. Thanks for checking up on me."

He remained frozen, his thin lips never moving from their straight line. I took a step back and tried to go back inside. But before I took that first step, he reached into his deep pocket and pulled out a gun.

And he was aiming right at me.

"Oh, shi—!"

There was a loud *BOOM!* and a sharp pain in my stomach. Unspeakable agony coursed through the rest of my body. I pressed my palm to my stomach and brought up my hand.

Blood. My hand was covered with blood.

My eyes rolled to the back of my head as I lost the energy to keep my legs up. The rain continued to pour down on me as peaceful blackness swallowed me whole.

CHAPTER NINETEEN

"Erin. Wake up, Erin."

I opened my eyes. A sharp pain stabbed my chest as I tried to breathe. My head felt heavy, filled with a fog that wouldn't dissipate. But despite all of this, there was one indisputable fact. *I'm alive.*

"Good," a deep, gruff voice said. "You're awake."

I rubbed my eyes and shot up. A dark green tent surrounded me, the "walls" lined with old tapestries and equipment, painting pictures of a foreign culture.

"Shh," a wrinkled hand gently shoved me back down. "You are still not healed. You must rest."

An old man sat in front of me. Wrinkles lined his face, telling stories of his experiences and wisdom. His gentle, sky blue eyes shone with empathy and care. His hair had balded long ago, leaving behind only sparse white strands. His body was covered with a long green cloak, a thick red sash draped across his chest.

And the vine-like tattoos of Mages ran up his neck and across his left cheek.

"I understand you are confused, Erin," he said, smiling. "Yes, I know your name. And yes, I am a Mage." He placed a hand on his chest. "I am Odyn. This is the Mage colony at Dover." He dipped a circular piece of cloth into a purple liquid and dabbed it on my stomach.

"Agh!" I shouted, arching my back in pain. "Son of a bitch!"

"I understand you are hurting," he said. "But this is necessary for your healing. You are very blessed to have such a kind and courageous friend. If she had not brought you here when she did, you would have surely died on those steps."

I smiled. "Charly is so sweet," I said, gritting my teeth as he dabbed the sponge on my wound once again.

Odyn frowned. "I do not know any Charly," he said.

I raised an eyebrow. "Then who was it?"

The front flap of the tent opened, letting in a bright beam of sunlight for only a moment. A young woman in deep red and gold robes walked in, her long, dark hair flowing behind her. My jaw dropped.

"Aya?"

"Ah," Odyn said. Aya knelt as he planted a kiss on her cheek. "My child. Thank you for bringing her here."

"How is she doing?" she asked, her voice filled with concern. *Since when does Aya ever care about me?*

"She is doing much better," he replied. "She has a fiery tongue, that is for sure."

Aya chuckled. "That's Erin for you," she laughed.

Odyn stood up, his aged joints creaking. "I must tend to other matters," he said, lifting the flap. "Can you finish healing her?"

Aya bowed her head. "Yes, Shaman."

"Thank you very much, my child." Odyn left, leaving Aya and me in the darkness of the tent.

I stared her down skeptically. "Okay, what the hell is all of this about?" I asked, my voice as sharp as a dagger. "First, you threaten my life, and then you save my life? I want answers!"

Aya nodded. "You're right," she said, her voice thick with guilt.

I opened my mouth to spit more harsh words at her, but stopped. "Wait—what?"

Aya sighed. "You're right. Well, Armyn was right."

I tried to sit up again, but the stabs of pain in my chest made me regret the attempt. "Who's Armyn?"

Aya dug into the folds of her robe. She pulled out a weathered piece of papyrus and handed it to me. I examined the portrait, and I finally realized why Aya was so familiar.

The Mage that day at the riot. The one who first told me *be not afraid.*

Aya looked just like her.

"Armyn was my twin sister. We grew up here in this village. Our parents died when we were young, during a raid by radical Chemists, so we really only had each other. We were both taken in by Odyn, the Shaman of our village, and we became his apprentices. But I always knew that Armyn was special. She could see the past, present, and the future. Our people called her *Noryne Mine*, which means 'Book of Truth' in our native tongue. Many of the things she predicted came to pass. Ten years ago, she predicted I was to become part of the Golgotha Project, and it happened. Even after we left, we still kept up with each other. I'd make regular visits back to the village to see her. I'd even bring her to London on special occasions. But she always preferred life here in the village.

"And then, several months ago, Armyn told me she was to deliver a message to a powerful but timid young woman in a town called New Washington. I expected it to be a quick journey. But then Odyn told me that she would never come home. Obviously, I was heartbroken. This woman could not have been worth my sister's life. So when you first came to the Golgotha

Project, I at best pretended you weren't there, and at worst, would envision ways to end your life.

"But then I saw you last night, in front of that wall. Armyn always talked about that wall, about how it needed to be broken. 'What has been done in darkness must be brought to the light,' she said. When I saw you crying in front of the opened wall, your hands singed and your lab coat on the ground, I just knew that Armyn was right about you. When you started running, I tried to follow you. And then I heard that gunshot. I saw you lying and bleeding on the ground. I healed you as best as I could with my magic, and brought you here." She took my hands. "I want to help you. Whatever was behind that wall must have been important. I know that now. If there's anything I can do, please tell me."

Tears spilled from my eyes and cascaded down my face. "I'm so sorry," I sputtered, gripping her hands even harder. The pain from my gunshot wound still coursed through me, making me cry even harder. "I tried to save her. I really did."

Aya shook her head. "There's nothing you really could have done," she said. "She knew that she was going to her death. She sacrificed her life so what was done in darkness could be brought to the light. She sacrificed her life because she knew you were worth it." She laughed at herself. "I just should've trusted her judgment." She sighed.

"Now," Aya continued, her voice now more resolute, "it's time we moved on to the next phase of healing. I'm going to need you to remove your clothes from the waist up."

My eyebrows furrowed. "Wait, what—?"

"I'm not an idiot, Erin," she interrupted. "I've known you've been practicing magic for months now. You know how I know?" She knelt down and took one of my arms, placing her finger at the top of one of my scars.

146

"You see these scars?" she asked, tracing her finger down the vine-like scar tissue. "This is what happens when you can't control your magic. Or more precisely, when you don't protect yourself from it."

I frowned, confused.

"Magic is raw energy," Aya said, as if teaching a young child. "That energy comes from the Earth."

"Whenever I use magic," I interrupted, "it's like I can feel this hum inside me, like a second heartbeat."

"That's exactly what I mean," Aya replied. "But that energy is very powerful, and if it isn't controlled, and not used properly, it can leave devastating scars, both physically and mentally." She sighed again. "I'm guessing Damon told you about Emily?"

I raised an eyebrow. "Yeah, he did."

"Damon took Emily's death pretty hard," Aya said mournfully. "Sweet girl. Smart, too. But I saw the scars on her arms, despite her best efforts to hide them; she was practicing magic in her free time. Overtime, the constant use of magic made her paranoid; Dr. Sharpe considered letting her go at one point. But Damon was so in love with her, he convinced Dr. Sharpe to let her stay, and that he would figure out what was wrong.

"Emily was found dead the next morning. Officially, the records say she burned to death in a lab accident, but I saw Emily's body before the Silent Ones took her away. Those were burns from magic. She had burned herself to death in an effort to learn more about her magic, to control it.

"Like Emily, you have the capability to be a powerful Mage. But practice isn't enough."

She lifted the sleeve of her robe on her right arm. The signature black vine-like tattoos of the Mages ran up her arm. "Do these look familiar?"

I stared at the tattoos, how they wound around her arm. *Wait a second...* I looked down at my own arm and examined my scars. They were the same shape and everything, down to the way they coursed over my body... like *vines.*

"My scars look just like your tattoos!"

Aya nodded. "In Mage villages, after a child shows the first signs of magical capabilities, they are given these special markings." She gestured to her arms. "The ink in these tattoos is made from a mixture of different plants and is blessed by the village's Shaman. The tattoos prevent any further damage from the raw energy, strengthen the power of the magic, and even provide some healing capabilities, depending on the types of plants used in the ink.

"If you keep practicing magic," she continued, concerned, "I'm afraid you'll end up like Emily. I don't want something like that to happen again. I won't let Armyn's sacrifice be in vain.

"You're going to get these tattoos, Erin, whether you like it or not."

My jaw dropped. "You're serious?"

"I'm more serious than I've ever been," Aya replied. I stared into her eyes as they radiated a sharp yellow and red, a slow, throbbing pain spreading from my own eyes through my head. "In fact, it's one of the reasons I brought you here. Now take off your clothes from the waist up. I'll go get the Shaman." With that, she left the tent, leaving me in the darkness.

The tattoos. I was going to be marked as a Mage. What would Mother and Father think? If someone was able to find these markings as easily as Aya was, then what about once the ink had settled in? I would be disowned! I would never see my Mother and Father again! And what if the Supreme Leader caught me?

But the way Aya's eyes stared me down as she told me of the tattoos' purpose, how they would help me, keep me safe... the way they glowed yellow and red...

there was no way she could lie. Her aura proved she was telling the truth. And if these tattoos really could help me, then why the hell not? I reached down to the buttons on my torn, blood-stained shirt, wincing as I removed the white cloth, then my nude bra.

Aya walked back in with Odyn following closely behind her.

"Now tell me, Erin," Odyn said as he knelt down in front of three straw barrels. "What has happened with your magic? Tell me everything. You are in safe hands here; no one else will know."

I swallowed. "Sometimes," I began nervously, "when I feel a certain strong emotion, the temperature around me will change. And not just body temperature; people notice and comment on it.

"During the riot in New Washington, the one where Armyn was killed"—my voice echoed with regret; the pain of the memory was clear on Aya's face—"I caused an explosion.

"And lately, when I've been practicing magic"—I held up my arms, showing him my scars—"I've been creating fire. Sometimes different things, but it's mostly fire."

Odyn nodded. "I see," he said thoughtfully. "It is clear that you are an Elemental."

"A what—?" I asked, confused.

"An Elemental—one who can wield the power of the Earth, manipulate the natural world." He turned back to the straw barrels in front of him. "Now that I know this, I can find the herbs I need for the spell." He opened the lid of the straw barrel closest to me and reached in. The sound of crinkling glass and clay echoed in my ears as he rummaged around the vessel's contents. "Edelweiss, zinnia..." he mumbled to himself. "Lilies—no, no, that will not do." I tilted my head in confusion, not understanding a single word he was saying. *Edelweiss?*

149

"Ah," Odyn said, a knowing smile spreading across his face, "here we are." He pulled out several glass jars, each filled with small, colorful flowers, grasses, and herbs, and laid them in a line next to him. He then reached in the baskets again, this time taking out a small, brown clay bowl and mortar, a tall candle on a black metal stand, a dagger no longer than my hand, and a small vial of mysterious gold liquid.

"Seal the tent tightly, my child," Odyn said softly to Aya. "We must not have any disturbances." Aya nodded, tying the opening shut with a small but thick leather rope which coiled through the flaps of the tent like twin snakes. The interior became shrouded in silent darkness. Only the sounds of our breathing could be heard.

"Now," he said to me, his eyes intense, "lay down. We can begin."

CHAPTER TWENTY

"In the beginning," Odyn said, his voice seeming to echo throughout the thick darkness of the tent, "there was only blackness, emptiness. There was no form, no hope. But a single word brought a new beginning.

"Light."

Just as the word escaped his lips, the single flame of the candle illuminated the room. Odyn had moved in the dark, and was now kneeling next to me. A total of nine jars encircled him. A hollowed-out bone which curved like an old horn or a saber tiger's tooth rested on his left. The now lit candle sat on his right. The brown bowl and mortar was in front of him, blackened and chipped from years of use. Aya remained by the door, as if guarding the entrance.

"And with the coming of light, so day was formed," Odyn continued. "But Dust dominated all things: the earth, the sky, the sea. And so it is said that in the ancient days, the creatures of the earth and the sky and the sea were created from that Dust.

"Just as it was then, so it is today, as you shall be created anew from the Dust of the earth."

Odyn reached over and opened the first jar to his far left. He pulled out a small stem covered with the tiniest of white flowers, his eyes never leaving mine.

"Baby's breath," he said, holding the plant to his face, "for innocence and purity of heart." He took the clay bowl and dropped the delicate flower inside it. He picked up the mortar and began to grind the plant into dust, the grating sound of clay against clay ringing in my ears. He set the bowl down again and reached into the second jar, this time pulling out a much larger white flower, its petals swirling around each other in a never ending cycle of beauty.

"The white carnation," Odyn said, "for all things sweet and lovely." He repeated the process of grinding the flower with the bowl and mortar. I snuck a look at the contents of the bowl as he lowered it back down in front of him: a swirling collection of white, sprinkled with tints of green.

Odyn reached into the third jar and pulled out a twig covered in pink blossoms. Some had fully blossomed, while others were still the tiniest of buds.

"Cherry blossoms," Odyn continued, "for the pursuit of knowledge and the love of learning." Once again, he ground the plant into the bowl, now adding in beautiful shades of bright red and pink to the mixture.

"The Christmas rose," Odyn stated, pulling out what appeared to be a hollow rose, its gold stigma rising from the center like a fountain frozen in time, "for the relief of anxiety." He added the flower to the concoction.

I looked over at Aya, her eyes focused solely on Odyn and me, as if this ritual was the most important thing in the world right now. Her intense gaze burned into my skin, even though my blood seemed to freeze like ice. Wild anxiety overtook me, despite the promises of the Christmas rose. The pain from my still slightly fresh gunshot wound didn't help, either. But something inside me seemed to remain calm, even in the face of the unknown. *Keep calm,* it seemed to tell me, my breaths slowing down with every passing second. *Everything is okay. Just keep breathing. In... out...*

"If you are anxious," Odyn said concernedly, "we can stop. You do not have to do this."

I shook my head. "No," I replied resolutely, staring him right in his ancient blue eyes. "Keep going." I shot a glance over at Aya; a small smile quickly ran across her face.

"Very well then," Odyn responded. He opened the fifth jar directly in front of him and pulled out a small white flower. Its sharp petals extended outwards like the rays of the sun, the yellow anthers glistening in the candlelight.

"Edelweiss," he continued, a knowing light twinkling in his eye, "for courage." He dropped the edelweiss into the bowl and mashed it in with the other flowers, creating a white and gold powder with small sprinkles of green and pink.

Odyn took great care in opening the sixth jar. He slowly reached in and pulled out what appeared to be a very small cactus, no more than a few inches long. Fleshy gold stems spread out from the white flower like fireworks. "Dragon root, for ardor," he said rather quickly, and equally as swift he dropped the cactus into the bowl. He took extra care in grinding the plant before setting the dish down and opening the seventh jar.

"Fraxinella," he said, pulling out what was similar to a violet striped lily, "for the fire that burns within oneself and within the world." He ground the flower in the bowl, which now added a slight purple tint to the otherwise predominantly white and gold mixture.

"The iris, for faith and wisdom," he went on and opened the eighth jar, the dainty purple plant resting in his hand. Three petals were outstretched like a trinity of beauty, a yellow stripe marking them as unique from the rest of the flower. He placed it into the bowl and ground it together into a fine powder with the rest of the plants.

"Lastly," Odyn stated, his voice clearer than it was before, "the scarlet zinnia, for constancy." He reached into the ninth and final jar and took out a round red flower. Its round petals circled around the bright yellow center in an eternal dance. He put the plant in the bowl and mortar, and like with the other eight plants, ground it into dust until all that was left in the dish was a white and gold powder marked with vibrant shades of green, red, and pink.

Odyn pulled the small vial of gold liquid from his pocket and opened it. A thin yellow mist rose from the top as he opened it. He picked up the bowl and poured two drops of the mysterious substance into it. The gold swirled around with the remains of the plants like the churning waves of the ocean, mixing and reacting with them until only a fine gold powder remained. "And it was thus," Odyn proclaimed as he raised the bowl above his head, "that the Dust of the Earth was gathered by the Light.

"But Light and Dust were not enough. For Life to spring forth, it needed a third element: *Breath*."

Odyn brought down the bowl and picked up the hollowed bone. He placed his finger at the smaller end of the bone and tilted the dish over the open end, allowing the gold dust to fall into it.

He put the now empty bowl down and turned to Aya. "My child," he said, his tone softening from the booming spiritualism that consumed him earlier, "I need your assistance."

Aya nodded silently as she crawled next to the circle of jars.

"Cut a hole right here, please," he said matter-of-factly. He took his empty hand, turned my left arm to where my wrist faced up towards him and placed his finger right at the center of my forearm.

"Wait, what!?" I shouted. "You're going to cut me!?"

"This is the last and most important part of the ritual," Odyn replied, his voice eerily calm. "Unfortunately, it is also the most painful."

"What are you going to do with that thing?" I asked anxiously, staring at the hollow bone.

"I am going to inject this ink into your arm," he answered. "The ink will then be absorbed into your bloodstream."

"Won't that kill me!?" I asked, feeling the temperature starting to fall around me. The anxiety that surged through me blocked off all of my rational thinking. Droplets of sweat ran down my face, my body stressed from the uncontrolled magic moving through me.

"Erin!" Aya shouted. "Erin, look at me!"

I turned my attention to Aya. Her eyes held my gaze, their intensity refusing to let me go. The sweat continued to fall down my face like tears. Her face burned with resolution, as if she was silently vowing that everything was going to be alright, once again delivering the message that Armyn had first given me.

Be not afraid.

I turned back to Odyn, breathing slowly yet deeply. "Go ahead," I said softly. My fear didn't fade away, but with Armyn's words echoing in my head, part of me just knew that I was going to be okay.

Odyn nodded slowly in return as his attention was once again fixed on Aya. "Cut here," he said simply, once again gesturing to the center of my forearm. She nodded, grabbing the small dagger he had pulled out earlier and crawling over to me. She rested the blade on my arm and stared at me, waiting for my cue. I nodded slowly and winced as she dragged the blade across my forearm. I could feel tiny drops of blood escape from beneath my skin and slide down the sides of my arm onto the cot. A stinging sensation shot through me as the open wound came into contact with the air.

Aya moved out of the way as Odyn inched the small end of the bone closer to the cut.

"Just as in the ancient days, when Breath created the first creatures from Dust and Light"—I groaned as he barely inserted the small end of the bone into the cut—"so shall I give to thee the Breath of Life." With that, Odyn blew into the bone, his breath echoing against the instrument like roaring wind in the silence of the tent.

My forearm tingled, the dust seeming to graze my skin as it entered my bloodstream. The area around my cut began to throb, accompanied by a dull ache. But as seconds passed, the beating sped up and spread up the rest of my arm, the pain growing sharper. I bit my lip as a sharp pang hit my shoulder, coursing through my veins up my neck, over my chest... *My head... it hurts...* I kept biting harder, fighting the urge to scream, until the metallic taste of blood hit my tongue.

"Ahhh!"

My screams echoed throughout the tent. The pain circulated through my chest to my heart, pounding faster and faster until I thought it would burst. It slowly flowed down until it hit my gunshot wound. "Ahhh!" My throat burned from my cries of agony, my chest, my arms... *Everything burns...* I gripped the blankets, tears welling in my eyes and falling down my face.

"Erin!" Aya shouted, reaching over to me.

Odyn held her back. "Do not touch her," he commanded as he stared at me warily. "You will only hurt her more."

I continued to scream as everything vanished into a white mist.

I open my eyes, breathing heavily. My chest and arms are still throbbing... but there's no pain. As I look around the white vacuum, a revelation dawns on me.

My dreams.

I start walking slowly. If I'm in this dream world again, *I think,* then the gold mist should be here.

"Hello!" I call out, my voice echoing through the vast emptiness. Nothing appears. I try calling out again. "Is anyone there?" Still nothing.

Just as I am about to give up hope, I hear a faint rustling coming from behind me. I turn around and look up, smiling.

The gold mist.

"Hello," I repeat, the gold anomaly settling in front of me. The entity swirls in greeting.

"Can you tell me what I'm doing here?" I ask. "I haven't been here in a long time."

The vapor continues to float before me, as if ignoring my question.

I frown. It hasn't acted like this before. *"What am I doing here?" I ask again. "One minute I'm at Dover receiving my Mage tattoos, and now I'm here. Did I pass out from the pain? Am I dead?"*

The mist stops moving completely, as if frozen in time. But suddenly a bright light encompasses it, blinding me. I raise my arm in front of my eyes, shielding myself from the glare. The throbbing in my body grows faster. As the light eventually fades, I begin to hear a quiet song, a second heartbeat. I move my arm down and gasp.

The entity had taken on a new form.

Me.

It—she—looks just like me. The plain brown hair, the green eyes. But there were several clear differences. She radiates a bright gold aura unlike anything I had ever seen. She wears a white dress that stretches down to her ankles underneath a lab coat. But this lab coat was different. It had no emblem on its breast pocket. The sleeves had been torn off, showing off thick black tattoos that wound up her arm and neck until they ended right at her jaw line. As I gather my hair behind my ears, I furrow my eyebrows as I notice that she does the same. I take that same hand and waved; once again, she copies my motions perfectly. I dare to look down at myself.

I look just like her: the tattoos, the torn lab coat, the white dress.

Everything's the same.

I look back up at her, my eyes wide. She smiles at me, her eyes radiating pride and dignity. She raises her hand in front of me, her palm extended towards me. Slowly, I raise my own hand towards hers. As we connect, she dissipates, a white light once again consuming everything.

I opened my eyes slowly again. I was back in the tent. The radiant colors of the sunset shone through the open doors. Aya sat opposite me, staring at me.

"Look who's back in the world of the living," she said with a chuckle.

I took a deep breath as I woke up. "How long have I been out?" I asked.

"A few hours," she replied, smiling. "How do you feel?"

I sat up, but then froze. *I shouldn't even be able to move.* But the more I thought about it, the more I realized that the pain had vanished, including that of my gunshot wound. I was alert, focused. I look down at my still exposed chest. Black vines stretched up my stomach and around my arms.

The tattoos.

"Congratulations," Aya said. "You're now officially a Mage."

158

A Mage. The words rang in my head, foreign yet comforting. But what about my science? I had come so far in my skills as a Chemist; did I have to throw all of that away? But then I remembered what Odyn had said during the ritual. *For the love of all things learning.*

I didn't have to stop learning, or sharing that knowledge with others.

And right now, I couldn't afford to.

"I know why New Pangaea has been having so many power outages."

Aya's head shot up, her eyes tense. "Was that what was behind the wall?"

I nodded. "The Gears aren't fully powered by kinetic energy like we thought," I said. "The magnetic field around Earth powers a core inside the Gears. That's what causes them to move."

"So?" Aya asked. "What does that mean?"

"It means the Gears don't provide an infinite amount of energy," I replied. "If you try to power too many things at once with them, the Gears will short-circuit and stop moving completely.

"But the question is, what is the source of these outages? What is making the Gears slow down?"

"I don't know," she replied, sighing.

I gulped, still nauseous over the two bodies I had found. "That's not all I saw," I said quietly.

Aya frowned. "What's wrong?" she asked.

I cleared my throat, attempting to fight back the urge to vomit. "I also found two skeletons. They both wore lab coats. However, one of them had an old Mage's robe underneath it, as if someone wore the lab coat over it." I swallowed. "On the pockets were the names *T. Luciani* and *E. Luciani*. My parent's names are Tom and Evelyn Luciani. T and E."

Aya's eyes widened. The blood drained from her face. "Oh, no," she whispered. She looked at me. "We have to get you out of here!" she shouted. "Put your clothes back on, and get up! You're not safe here!"

"What do you mean?" I asked, frowning as I threw my shirt back on.

"You don't understand!" she cried desperately as we exited the tent. "We have to get you somewhere safe before they—!"

"Before who does what?"

A clear, familiar voice rang in my ears. I squinted at the white form as my eyes adjusted to the sunlight.

"Dr. Sharpe," Aya said nervously. "What are you doing here?"

"Why, checking on you and Miss Erin, of course," he replied. "When neither of you showed up for breakfast this morning, I was concerned. I cannot have my colleagues disappear; that would endanger the mission. Allow me to take Miss Erin," he added, his voice carrying a slightly commanding edge.

Aya stepped back, guarding me defensively. I squeezed her arm. "It's okay," I said. "We can trust Dr. Sharpe. Just tell Odyn I'm going back to London."

Aya furrowed her eyebrows. "Just remember I'm here to help," she said as she hesitantly moved out of the way.

"You are doing the right thing, Miss Aya," Dr. Sharpe said. "I will meet you back at Headquarters. We can talk more then."

Aya swallowed. "Yes, sir," she replied, her gaze never leaving us as we walked away.

Dr. Sharpe looked at me. "Now, Miss Erin," he said as I followed him to the familiar black car. "I will take you back to Headquarters. But first, I need to speak with you. It is urgent that we discuss this matter as soon as possible." He placed me in the back seat of the car and climbed in next to me. "Just to make sure no one intrudes," he said, locking all of the doors. He turned to me, his eyes staring me down.

"I have not been completely honest with you," he said. "I was not on a tour of New Pangaea. I did not choose you for the reasons that I originally said." He gently grasped my hand. "You are someone who is very important to New Pangaea." His expression began to contort as his grip on me grew tighter.

"Ow," I said, wincing. He firmly turned my wrist to where it faced him. "What are you doing!?" I shouted.

He used his other hand to bring out a syringe filled with a clear liquid. "You are someone who is very important to New Pangaea." He stabbed me with the needle and pressed down, releasing the drug into my system. The world around me began to fade. It was like I had been shot all over again.

"And someone who is very dangerous."

CHAPTER TWENTY-ONE

"Good morning, honey."

Joy filled my heart as I heard her voice.

"Mother," I mumbled, my voice slurred, "I had an awful dream that I had magic, and I was taken away from you, and I was shot, and..."

"Honey," Father said. "That wasn't a dream."

My eyes shot wide open. Dark brick walls surrounded me, and the only light came from a dim, flickering fixture above me. I was on my knees, my arms held up as if I were nailed to a cross. I tried to move them, but couldn't. I looked up at them, and saw they were held up by chains. I tried to stand up, but fell down due to the pain in my chest and the vertigo brought on by drugs. I looked up, hoping to see the familiar faces of my mother and father.

But the two figures before me weren't them. They couldn't be them. Their eyes were blocked by thick black lenses. Their black suits blended in with the dark, dank walls of the cell. "Good morning," the woman repeated. They even had their voices. But these people—these *things*—couldn't be the loving faces I grew up with.

These things were Silent Ones.

"Where are my parents!?" I shouted angrily, fighting against the chains.

"They've been dead for twenty years."

That voice. I had only heard it once before, but it still rang familiar in my ear. I turned my head towards the sound. There she stood, her blond locks cascading down her doll-like face.

LaVanna.

But she wasn't alone. A young man in a white lab coat stood beside her, his dark hair pulled back into a ponytail. He stared me down with his intense eyes. My jaw dropped, and my heart broke.

"Dr. Sharpe..." I barely managed to choke out. "W...what are you...?"

"It is all part of the mission, Miss Erin," he said, withdrawing his gaze.

"Mission?" I asked. "What mission? What's going on? What are you all doing here? Why am I chained to this cell? *Where are my parents!?*"

"As I said, Miss Erin," LaVanna replied, "they have been dead for twenty years. You are Erin Luciani, but these two people whom you have called Mother and Father for twenty years—they are not Tom and Evelyn Luciani."

"Then who are they?" I snarled.

"We are no one," Mother replied. "We have no names."

"That makes no sense!" I shouted.

"Ah, but it makes perfect sense," LaVanna said. "Your real parents—the real Tom and Evelyn Luciani—were once members of the Golgotha Project. Tom was a Chemist. Evelyn was a Mage. Against the moral codes of New Pangaea, they fell in love, and married in secret. Evelyn then gave birth to a child—*you.* They tried their hardest to hide Evelyn's pregnancy. But nothing can escape my watchful eye. I had them murdered by two of my agents"—she gestured to Mother and Father—"but they figured you would be useful. So I gave them voices, personalities, and allowed them to raise you as their own."

"But that was twenty years ago," I said. "You would've only been what, two years old? There's no way you would be this young if you were the one who commanded the—" My eyes widened. An alarm of realization rang in my head. I stared at the wires on LaVanna's face. "You," I said quietly.

"You're the one who's siphoning the energy from the Gears. You're using the energy to keep yourself young."

LaVanna brought back her curls behind her ears, showing off the bronze anodes. "New Pangaea needs a Supreme Leader to guide her," she said.

I shook my head. "But you're not the Supreme Leader," I replied. "Your Father is."

"There is only one Supreme Leader," she said, her voice edged with anger. "And that is me."

"But the Supreme Leader was always described as a great Man—"

"My father was not great!" LaVanna snarled. "He was a drunkard, a cheat and a murderer! He beat my mother to death in a drunken rage, all because she tried to use her magic to heal his wounds from an accident in the lab! I was there. I remember. I remember my mother's cries of agony, the sound of bones and cartilage crunching under his fists, her hands reaching out for help. I saw it *all*. Do you know what it's like to watch someone die? To see the last signs of life leave their bodies? And when he was done, when he saw me, I knew he was going to kill me. I desperately crawled away from him as he stumbled towards me, his drunkenness clouding his senses. I looked up and saw a shotgun on the wall—his favorite shotgun. In desperation, I reached up and grabbed it off the wall. Just as he was over me, I shot him in the heart. Blood spattered everywhere as he collapsed to the floor.

"I was seven years old when that happened, but I knew at that point that Chemists and Mages could not be together, that they must be kept separate. No one else would understand like I did. I assumed the position of Supreme Leader. As years passed, my body began to age. No one else could care for New Pangaea like I could. I had built these anodes to keep myself young, yes. But I keep myself young for the good of New Pangaea. Nothing good can come from the mix of science and magic."

"We have nothing to do with what happened," I said, my arms tingling from being held up. "Chemists and Mages can be together. Just look at the Golgotha Project itself. Led by a Chemist, but relying on the collaborative efforts of Chemists and Mages. Times are changing, LaVanna. We will all be treated equally one day. There is no Mage or Chemist; we're all human. We're all members of this global nation."

"But look at the riots in the streets!" LaVanna spat. "Look at the death and destruction caused by their hatred!"

"Hatred you plant in them," I replied. "If the people were equal, these riots wouldn't happen in the first place."

"*Silence!*" she screamed, her voice becoming more and more desperate. "I have had enough of you." She turned to Dr. Sharpe and the Silent Ones. "She will be dead by sundown; is that clear?" They nodded in unison as they all exited the cell, leaving me alone in the damp darkness.

I bowed my head. Never had I felt so alone, so broken. *Mother... Father... Dr. Sharpe... I've really lost everything.* Pain radiated from every part of my body. Was everything I went through really worth it? *I'm going to be dead in a matter of hours.* I sighed. *At least Aya knows what's wrong with the Gears. Maybe she can fix it.*

I closed my eyes and whispered a silent prayer before drifting off to sleep once more—

The door of the cell creaked open.

My head shot up. Was it really my time to die already? I narrowed my eyes defensively as the male Silent One knelt down in front of me.

"LaVanna has commanded me to kill you," he said. "She says you are a danger to New Pangaea."

"I know this," I spat. "So just get it over with already."

He furrowed his eyebrows, then brought his attention to the chains. He took an old key out of his pocket and released me.

I breathed deeply as the blood rushed through my arms. "You're... you're saving me?" I asked, rubbing my wrists where the shackles once were.

He looked deep into my eyes. "We are not supposed to be capable of love," he said. "At first, you were nothing more than a mission. But your eyes shone with a kind of passion that I had never seen before. Because of you, I believed that there was good in the world. I lied to LaVanna when I told her why I wanted to keep you. I didn't want to kill you. So I raised you as my own. I may not be the real Tom Luciani, but you are my Erin. And I will not kill my daughter."

I narrowed my eyes. "How do I know this isn't some trap?" I asked. "There's probably a horde of Silent Ones out there, waiting for me to walk out of this cell."

"I know you probably don't trust me," he replied, "especially after I lied to you for so long. But right now you have two options: wait in here to die, or take my advice."

I continued rubbing my wrists. "Let's say I do take your advice," I said, refusing to address him as my Father. "What do I do?"

"Orpheus, Charly, Damon, Aya, and Vynessa are all waiting for you outside," he said. "I called them as soon as I learned that Dr. Sharpe brought you here."

I stood up, still surprised at the healing powers of the tattoos.

"Let's just go," I spat, walking out the door.

As I stepped out of my cell, a loud alarm echoed through the building.

I glared at the Silent One. "You lied to me!"

"You need to go!" he shouted, ignoring my accusation. "They'll be here any minute!" He pointed behind me. "There's a secret exit that way. You'll see a small staircase going down. Keep going until you get out of this Tower. Just get out! Now!" He shouted as he ran down the hall and vanished from my view.

I ran away as quickly as I could towards the door, and down a winding staircase. I could hear the thundering footsteps of the Silent Ones growing louder behind me.

"Shit," I swore to the rhythm of my breathing. I kept running, down the steps, until I saw a light ahead of me. *Finally! I can get out—*

There was nothing but a moat below me.

Now what do I do!? I could hear Silent Ones closing in on me from all sides. *If I go to the left, I'm dead. If I go to the right, I'm dead. If I jump off, I won't be killed by LaVanna, but I'll probably be dead, anyway.*

The Silent Ones grew closer and closer.

I looked down at the moat. It didn't seem too far down. I sighed. *I guess I have nothing left to lose!* I let go of my apprehension and jumped off the wall of the Tower. I could feel gravity pulling my body down to the water, but my spirit seemed to fly higher and higher. Peace fell on me like a steady April shower...

And then I hit the water like a rock.

The brown, muddy water covered me as I was submerged in the moat. The water ran up into my nostrils and down my throat. I desperately tried to swim to the top, my chest growing tighter and tighter from the lack of oxygen.

The crisp evening air filled my lungs as I broke the surface. *I'm alive!* I thought victoriously. I sighed. *There's still LaVanna and her Silent Ones, though.*

"Erin!" I heard Orpheus' voice call out. I looked around, trying desperately to find him. "Up 'ere!" I looked up, and there he was, sitting on top of the outer wall of the Tower, along with Dr. Vermaak, Damon, Charly, and Aya. He threw down one end of a rope. "Climb!"

I grabbed onto the rope. Orpheus and the others grabbed onto the other end. "Hold tight!" Charly said. I gripped the rope for dear life as I was up out of the moat and onto the wall.

Damon wrapped his arms around me. "You're much stronger than I ever knew, Erin," he said, a genuine smile running across his face. I mirrored his goofy smile with my own. But then Damon frowned.

"Is something wrong?" I asked quizzically.

His eyes widened and his jaw dropped in alarm. "Everyone, get down!"

He pushed me down, my face against the stone wall, his firm grip never leaving the back of my head. A loud *BOOM!* rang in my ears, followed by the sound of tearing flesh. Damon's grip loosened. I tried to look up, but Charly pressed her hand against my back.

"Stay down!" she commanded as she flung a fireball from her hand. The death scream of a man several yards behind me echoed in the twilight.

As I sat back up, I noticed Damon was hunched over, one hand supporting him on the wall, and the other wrapped around his chest. A red stain grew larger under his hand. He looked back up at me, his eyes filled with pain and surprise.

"Get him off the wall!" Dr. Vermaak said. "Now!"

Orpheus gathered the wounded man in his arms as he climbed down a ladder that had been propped up next to him on the wall. Everyone else followed him down.

Damon groaned in pain, holding his wounded side even tighter. "'e's been shot!" Orpheus shouted. "What do we do!?"

"He's bleeding out too fast!" Aya shouted desperately. "I don't have enough time! Does anyone have any bandages!?"

"Stop..." Damon said weakly. "It's okay." He looked me dead in the eyes, holding out his hand. "Emily..."

The eyes of every person around me welled up with tears. "Emily's not..." Dr. Vermaak began...

"No," I interrupted. I knelt down next to him and held his hand. "I'm here."

A peaceful smile lined his face. "Emily..." he spluttered, blood trickling out of his mouth. "I love you... so much..."

"I know," I said, my eyes welling with tears. "I love you, too."

His smile grew bigger. "Really?" he asked. "That makes me so happy. But I'm so tired... can I have a kiss good night?"

I nodded. "Of course." I leaned down and gingerly kissed him, the salty, metallic taste of blood crossing my lips. "I'll see you in the morning."

"I'll see you in the morning," Damon repeated, the light of his eyes fading like the light of a candle.

Orpheus knelt down and slid his hand down Damon's face, closing his eyes.

The roaring wind was the only noise around us. First Armyn, now Damon had died in front of me. All because of me. "There's no way I'm worth all of these lives," I whispered, wiping the tears from my eyes.

Charly placed a hand on my shoulder. I looked up at her. Her eyes filled with empathy.

"Erin has a plan," Aya said, her expression stern.

"Really?" Dr. Vermaak asked.

Everyone's attention focused on me. Now was the time to not be afraid.

"Yes," I said. "The Gears aren't powered by kinetic energy. Earth's magnetic field helps power a core inside of them. But if you try to use too much power, the Gears will short-circuit and stop moving. If my hypothesis is correct, LaVanna has been siphoning this energy to essentially keep herself immortal. If we can stop the Gears, we can stop LaVanna."

Charly raised her hand. "But how do we—?"

A faint rustling noise echoed from behind us. A Silent One reached out of the bushes, her long arms reaching around Charly and pulling her close. Charly's eyes widened as the Silent One slit her throat, blood spewing out like a fountain. She brought her hands to her throat to close the wound with magic, but the blood pumped out too fast. She collapsed to the ground,

"No!" Dr. Vermaak cried, falling to her knees and gathering Charly's body in her arms. "Please! Please!" she prayed.

The Silent One reached for Dr. Vermaak, but a pair of hands reached out from behind her. A loud *CRACK!* rang through the air as the hands broke her neck. I peered into the shadows, trying to get a glimpse of the person who killed the Silent One.

Dr. Sharpe stepped through the bushes.

CHAPTER TWENTY-TWO

"What are you doing here!?" I snapped, standing defensively in front of Damon's and Charly's bodies. "Shouldn't you be with LaVanna right now? Shouldn't you be following the 'mission?'"

Dr. Sharpe shook his head. "The mission is to protect the Gears from those who would misuse its power," he said simply. "But now that I have learned who and what our Supreme Leader really is, I cannot in good conscience continue to support LaVanna in her reign." He knelt down in front of me. "Please accept my humblest apologies for the way I have treated you. Not just today, but since the first day I met you. I am willing to help you in whatever way I can. I have led this Project for many years, and I have information about the Gears that you do not. I would highly recommend that you take advantage of this opportunity."

"Tell him to go fuck himself!" Aya snarled. "He knows how much pain he has caused. Besides, he's probably just trying to get information from us to give to LaVanna."

"You killed her," Dr. Vermaak whimpered, rocking Charly's body back and forth as if she were a sleeping baby. "You killed Damon."

"I really don't like the idea of working with 'im again," Orpheus said. He turned to me. "But it's your call. You're the one who's figuring this out."

Everyone, Dr. Sharpe included, eyed me expectantly. I closed my eyes.

Be not afraid.

"Alright, Dr. Sharpe," I said, staring at him. "I'll let you help us. But if one more person dies, or if I find out you're still working with LaVanna, I'll let Aya end your sorry life."

Dr. Sharpe bowed his head. "I would not dream of it." He stood up. "And please, call me Makswell," he added quietly. "Now, I heard you discussing your plan. It is a simple plan, indeed. But if we are to stop the Gears, we have to make it back to Headquarters."

"And how are we going to do that?" Aya asked, eyeing him skeptically.

"With that." Dr. Sharpe pointed behind us. We turned around. There in front of us sat the black car, the one that Orpheus had driven when I first arrived in London. "Now, LaVanna has declared Erin an enemy of the state," he said as we followed him towards the car. "By helping her, you are all putting yourselves in great danger. You understand this, correct?"

Everyone nodded.

"Very well, he continued. "There will be Silent Ones everywhere. If we are to make it to Headquarters unnoticed, I will need to hide all of you." He opened the trunk and pulled out a set of blankets. "You will need to hide between the seats and be covered with these blankets. It will not be enjoyable, but this new mission is not about enjoyment, but ending tyranny." He opened the door to the back seat. Orpheus, Dr. Vermaak, and Aya looked at each other and nodded as we climbed into the car, grunting as we tried to fit all of us into the cramped back seats.

"We will be there shortly," Dr. Sharpe— Makswell—said as he placed the covers over us.

******

"LaVanna has asked me to return to Headquarters to acquire some documents for her," Makswell said.

The uncomfortable car ride felt like an eternity. Dr. Vermaak's foot stabbed me right in my gunshot wound. I had to bite my lip until it bled to stop myself from screaming. The thick, rough blankets only made the car ride that much worse.

"Very well," I flinched as I heard the voice of whom I once thought was my Mother. Dr. Vermaak softly stroked my hand with her own, her skin caked with Charly's blood.

The car slowly began to move again. I could hear the sounds of everyday city life coming from Makswell's open window. No one knew what was really happening. For everyone else, today was just an ordinary day.

The car came to a stop. I heard Makswell get out of the car and open the door.

"We do not have much time," he said as he removed the blankets. "We must move quickly." We quickly climbed out, the Headquarters towering above me. Makswell opened the door to the Headquarters and we ran inside as fast as we could.

He shut the door and locked it behind us. The place was completely dark. All of the lights and equipment were turned off. I looked up and recognized where we were. This was the door I came through when I first arrived in London. Nostalgia ran through me for a moment. But this was no time for memories.

"To stop the Gears, we need to power as many things as we can until the Gears wear out," he said. "I want everyone to split up and turn everything on that you come across. I do not care if it is a stove, or a holographic table or even the sprinklers. *Everything* must be turned on or else this will not work. We'll use our ArO-Ses to communicate.

"For the last time, I thank you for your service," Makswell said. "Now go! Remember, turn *everything* on!" Everyone else ran up the steps and split off into different directions. I started to run after them, but Dr. Sharpe pulled me back.

"Wait a moment, Miss Erin," he said, bringing me back down the steps.

"What is it?" I asked.

"I have a special task for you. We need a distraction while we power everything up here. I need you—*we* need you—to go out there and face her. Know that you may not come back alive. But also know that you are performing a great service that New Pangaea can never repay you for." He pressed his lips to my cheek. "Do not be afraid," he said.

"Trust me," I replied. "I won't be."

CHAPTER TWENTY-THREE

"Where are you, LaVanna!?" I shouted as I stepped out the door. "I know you're here. You want me!? You've got me!" Thunder rolled in the distance.

A whooshing sound echoed behind me, creating a harsh gust of wind. I turned around, covering my eyes so dust wouldn't fly in them. A small, grey cylindrical pod landed before me. The door opened and LaVanna walked out with her hands behind her back, clad in a slim black robe.

"You have no idea what you're doing, do you?" she asked, but her tone wasn't angry... just sad. She brought her hands out. In one hand she carried a sword, its hilt filled with arsenoformic acid. An orb of purple lightning hovered in the other hand. "You're blindly following the ravings of a madman."

"Dr. Sharpe is a genius," I retorted, as I started her down and breathed deeply, becoming aware of my heartbeat as it mixed with the heart of the earth, which in turn combined with the beat of the thunder. I grew stronger as adrenaline pumped through me, the rhythm of nature echoing around me like a battle hymn. Fire burned around both of my hands, but to my shock, it didn't hurt me. I looked down at my stomach.

My tattoos. They were glowing.

I looked back up at LaVanna. "Come at me, bitch," I snarled.

LaVanna's face contorted as she leapt towards me, her high-pitched screams ringing through the city. I ducked out of the way, hurling a fireball towards her. She dodged it gracefully and threw lightning at me. I held my hands up and brought them down to my sides, summoning a shield of fire to block her magic. *How am I able to do this?* I asked myself, dodging her attacks. *I've never had any experience fighting. It's just... instinct....* I had no time to question my intuition as I rolled away from her again.

She ran towards me, swinging her sword. As she brought it down and prepared to strike, I dodged her attack as the sword went down. I launched another fireball at her back as I landed. She screamed in agony as the fire burned through her robes and melted her skin.

I smiled. *Killing her is going to be easy.*

LaVanna's skin reformed and healed until it was as if nothing had happened in the first place.

My smile vanished. *Oh, shit.*

She turned to me, smiling maniacally like a serial killer ready for their next victim.

I rolled out of the way as she ran toward me. "How are we doing, guys?" I asked as I held up my ArO-S.

"We're going as fast as we can," Orpheus replied. *"But the Headquarters are huge. It'll take a while. You alright?"*

"Yeah, I'm fine," I said as I dodged the swings of LaVanna's sword one by one. "Just hurry up, okay?"

"Yes, ma'am," Orpheus said.

"You're making a huge mistake!" LaVanna shouted, her voice now more desperate than angry.

"I know *exactly* what I'm doing!" I countered as I brought up my right hand, this time launching a spiked ball of ice toward her. LaVanna broke it easily with her sword. I looked up longingly at the Gears, still spinning. *Please, everyone. Hurry.*

I made the fire wall again as she tried to strike me down with her sword. I pushed the wall towards her, engulfing her in flames. As the fires dissipated, she ran her hands across her head. All of her beautiful golden locks had been burned off.

My fire. *It's getting weaker.*

"Please, stop!" LaVanna shouted, almost begging.

I hid behind a car as she hurled herself at me. "Guys?" I asked, breathing heavily. Even with the blessed ink in my tattoos, it couldn't stop the pain and exhaustion that radiated through my body. I held up my ArO-S again. "How's Makswell doing?" No response. "Guys? Where's Makswell?"

"He's gone," Dr. Vermaak said slowly.

I stopped dead in my tracks. "What?"

"The only way to stop the Gears is to stop them manually. Makswell said he was 'taking matters into his own hands;' he left to stop them himself about twenty minutes ago."

Right when I left to fight LaVanna. "How long should it take him to get there?"

"We have the technology to get to the Gears in as little as fifteen minutes, Miss Erin," Makswell said, his voice broken by static. *"And I am already here.*

"Now, my friends. It is time for a new beginning."

An orb of purple lightning hit me in the shoulder, knocking me down. LaVanna walked over to me, her small frame seeming to tower over me as I lay on the pavement.

"I have to protect New Pangaea, Erin," LaVanna said, her sad eyes staring into mine. "If you won't listen to reason, then there's nothing I can do."

I closed my eyes, waiting for death to take me in his quiet arms.

But it never came.

I opened my eyes and looked up at LaVanna. Her face was contorted by electric shock and surprise. White and gold sparks jumped from anode to anode. Her body began to rapidly age, as if making up for the years she had siphoned the Gears' energy. She collapsed onto the ground.

"Wh—" she breathed, her once bright, youthful face now pale and wrinkled. "What have you done?" She let out one final breath, and the light in her eyes faded, leaving only darkness behind.

I breathed heavily. *I'm alive.* I looked up at the Gears.

They had stopped spinning.

"We did it!" I shouted, a huge grin lining my face. "We saved New—!"

That was when the screams started.

It was soft at first, distant even. I kept smiling. *They must be cheering.* But as the noise grew louder with every passing second, I frowned. The cries... they were too sad, too fearful to be cheers of joy. It was then I noticed that the entire street had gone dark. The lights from the buildings had switched off. Even the arms of the great clock had stopped counting time.

And then... sheer chaos.

The thunder roared as people ran out of the buildings in droves, screaming as they broke off into different directions. Lightning flashed as flying cars rained down from the sky, the resulting explosions setting the city ablaze. A young woman tripped over her own two feet and fell to the ground, seeming to vanish as the throng of panicked civilians ran over her. A small, bloody arm poked out from underneath the wreckage of what was once a flying car.

My throat became dry and my legs grew weak as the carnage unfolded before me. My voice was completely gone. I bent over as the urge to vomit overwhelmed me, the acidic muck spewing from my mouth onto the ground. I wiped off my mouth with my sleeve, my appearance the last thing on my mind, and took out my ArO-S.

"Makswell!" I shouted as his face materialized on the screen. "What's going on!?" I thought stopping the Gears would make everything better, save New Pangaea!"

"Yes," he replied, giddiness and joy oozing from his voice. "But New Pangaea must be burned, so that something even greater may rise from the ashes!"

"Erin!" Aya's voice echoed from behind me. I turned around; Aya, Orpheus, and Dr. Vermaak were all running out of the Headquarters towards me.

"Is everything okay!?" Dr. Vermaak shouted. "You're not wounded, are you?" She looked at Orpheus, his expression focused on the destruction in front of him.

"What 'appened 'ere?" Orpheus stammered, the blood draining from his face. "I thought Makswell was going to stop the Gears."

"He did," I replied, my voice shaking. "The Gears have stopped." I fell to my knees, a cold sweat overtaking me despite the hellish heat of the fiery city. The black night was illuminated by the infernal reds and oranges which engulfed the once glorious city. A rumbling, crackling sound echoed in my ears. As I turned to my right, I saw the great clock towering into the night sky for the very last time before it crumbled to the ground before the might of the flames. Just like Damon, Charly... those innocent lives I sacrificed because I fell for Makswell's lies.

Makswell was wrong. This wasn't a rebirth.

This was hell.

"Darwin," I choked out weakly. "What have I done?"

Acknowledgements

Wow. I never thought I would make it this far. I have so many people to thank.

First, there's Amy, who told me never to stop writing, and who coached me every step of the way in writing this book. Thanks for being patient with me.

To my fraternity sisters. I love you all!

And there's my family. We may be a crazy one, but I would never want another. I love you guys.

To everyone who helped make this possible. You know who you are.

But most of all, thank you, beautiful reader, for picking up this book. I hope you like it. You are awesome, and don't let anyone tell you otherwise.

About the Author

Rebekah McAuliffe has had a love of writing, coffee, and being crazy all of her life. She loves to write anything that strikes her fancy, drink tons of coffee, and cuddle with her cats. She can be found on Twitter, Facebook, her website and her blog, if she's not playing video games. She currently attends Morehead State University in pursuit of receiving a degree in education.

CPSIA information can be obtained
at www.ICGtesting.com
Printed in the USA
FFOW04n1610130316
22137FF